GIFTEN

GIFTEN

LEYLA
SUZAN

PUSHKIN PRESS

Pushkin Press
Somerset House, Strand
London WC2R 1LA

Giften was first published by Pushkin Press in 2021

3 5 7 9 8 6 4 2

ISBN 13: 978-1-78269-317-8

Designed and typeset by Tetragon, London

Printed and bound by Clays Ltd, Elcograf S.p.A.

www.pushkinpress.com

For E.B.

The dusty bowls and dishes lie
on tables oak and brown
But where did all the people go?
No children's merry sounds

I ask the winter, call the snow
to bring my mammy home
To fill the dishes on the table
with soft sweet-smelling loam

ANONYMOUS

My First Testimonial

I touch the pencil to my tongue as I have seen our Recorder do so many times, and begin to write down Logan's words, committing them to the rough paper sheets, to be read by people I will probably never meet.

It is impossible to feel anything but joy on a day like today. The Field, in the late summer sunshine, sparkles. I watch our friends bend to the task of repairing their cabins in time for the winter frost and the young ones collecting fat windfall from swollen apple trees, their mouths stained purple from gorging on blackberries. Their laughter trills through the Woods, even now, when you feel that your world is about to end.

My own story is a simple one, Ruthie.

My mother recorded the voices of our northern land and that job, on her death, fell to me. My own death, and yours, will not silence our stories. I record them for all who come after, so they will know we rejoiced as much as we suffered.

Do not forget they are the words of real people whose hands worked the earth and raised their children, whose voices hold within them every word of wisdom you will ever need, every comfort.

Is it lonely work? Tiring? Of course. But I ask for help and help is often given: willing hands keep the wheels of my old yellow solar turning; the papermakers are generous and there is a woman who crafts charcoal into sturdy pencils just for me.

I put away the idea of a One and Only a long time ago, when I was little more than a child. When your head is full of the lives of others, what can you offer of yourself? It might be different for you.

From the Lakes to the Hebrides, from the smallest communities to the vast; from inland, to the coasts and even to the City, and in all weather, I follow paths, tracks and cratered roads to gather stories as if they were pigment to paint a picture of our world. So much strength and resolve, so much despair and searing pain—all this will make a fine canvas of lives lived in constant renewal.

I'm not impartial. How can you record the resilience of our people and remain detached? Ever since the Darkening the challenges have been great. And I'm only human.

My ancestors witnessed the destitution of our land and also, its slow revival. While I rejoice in our growth, it is with grief that I have had to record the hunting of the Giften all these years and the tales of those who would protect them.

You have come to a fork in the road, Ruthie, and you will take the new path. You will see new things. And meet new people.

You listen well; maybe the life of a Recorder will suit you. Let this be your first record.

LOGAN—THE RECORDER

Prologue

Joshie was fourteen when the MAGs took him.

He was my favourite older boy when I was a smallie, we all wanted to play with him and he never chased us away. We laughed at his bad jokes and helped him with his chores when he would let us. His hair, the colour of wheat, had a way of flopping down over his eyes when he laughed. His smile revealed a dimple in one cheek.

In the weeks after, my dreams were strange, violent things. I'd wake up with lingering shouts of defiance ringing in my ears, still panting from dream-running through thick woodland, chasing after my friend who was being dragged away by men with guns.

But I didn't chase after him. I didn't do anything. No one did.

The edges of the thick forest circling our land were ankle deep with autumn leaves that day. Stace and I were playing, in the reds, yellows and golds, the sun glinting off everything it touched. She thought we were too old to *play* at eleven, but Joshie changed her mind about that when he nudged us into a game, chasing us further into the Woods. Hide and seek turned into catch-me-if-you-can, and soon enough we were all running around the Hollow Oak.

Stace caught me, tripped me up and she and Joshie began to pile on the leaves. I held still, because this was also part of the game. If you're caught, you get buried and then, you get to burst out like a thunderstorm. The smell of autumn leaves, the feel of the earth at my back, the sun on my skin—all of it as real as the moments that followed.

I was still under this crunchy blanket when I felt Stace's kick.

"Ruthie! Our mums are calling."

I scrambled, but she and Joshie were already running out of the Woods and into the Field. And there was Mum, shouting my name.

The sun was setting over the row of cabins, the sky full of pink. Wood smoke trailed out of our chimneys, curling, white. Stace was already halfway across the Field, bare legs paddling to keep up with her mum, but Joshie was waiting for me, one foot in the Woods, the other in the Field.

"What's going on?" I panted, bent double, hands on my knees. But Mum's eyes were on Joshie, not me.

"Run!" she shouted at him. "Get out of here!"

"What?" he said, taking a step.

"Joshie!" Amy, his mum, her face as red as the autumn leaves, streamed past Mum, folding him into her arms, her mouth at Joshie's ear, whispering urgent words. Mum's hand was tight around my arm as she started to run for the cabins.

"They've come for the Offering," she panted. "You need to get inside."

The MAGs were here.

Mum slowed down, dropping my arm as we passed the MAGs, their black solars parked outside Dev's cabin, next to ours.

Three MAGs; giant insects, in their uniforms of black. Their holstered guns and hard bodies made my heart bang harder. The adults were gathered around the solars; the MAGs were shouting, pointing at the hessian sacks of fresh veg, earthen containers of dried fruit and cloth-wrapped packets of smoked deer meat. The Offering—*our* food. But that summer had been especially good to us, the harvest was plenty enough to see us through the bad weather *and* to make the Offering. They should be happy, I thought, bitterly, but something else was going on here, something bad enough to make the mums call us home.

As I climbed the porch steps, Mum at my back nudging me to go faster, the voices grew louder. A very tall MAG stepped up to Dad, shouted into his face. I caught the word *Giften*.

"Stay inside!" Mum hissed and then she was gone.

From my bedroom window I watched the MAG aim his gun at the sun and fire. I covered my ears as everyone scattered. The crack bounced off the trees and the high peal of a baby's scream ripped through the air. Baby

Amaya was thrust above the heads of the small crowd by strong arms, MAG arms. She writhed and shrieked. The giant MAG swept his gun across the frightened faces of my community.

Joshie and his mum raced up their porch steps and slammed the door. The baby carried on squirming, screaming while Daisy, her mum, clawed at the MAG's arms.

"Let her go. Please!"

Everyone but the baby fell silent when the back door of a MAG solar swung open and from behind darkened windows a woman emerged.

I had never seen her before, but we all knew who she was. My heart had been thumping hard, but now it felt like it had stopped.

The first thing that struck me about her was how clean she was. Her clothes weren't made from other clothes sewn together like ours. She wore a pale blue shirt, a copper brooch pinned to a crisp collar; grey trousers with a sharp crease. Her red boots shone in the low afternoon sun. Even though she looked quite old, she had a young girl's hair, long, straight and yellow, which fell down her back, untroubled by the breeze.

"Let's all take a moment, shall we?" she said. Her voice was sweet, soothing. She gestured for the baby, holding out her arms.

"What's your name then?" she asked, cradling Amaya. The adults were silent. Dad's arm circled Mum's shoulders, drawing her close.

"Amaya. She's my daughter," Daisy said, through her sobs.

"And I'm Saige Corentin," she said. "Oh, come now. You don't have to be like that."

Defiant, unsmiling faces stared back at her.

Amaya had stopped crying; something about Saige Corentin had transfixed her.

"We came for the Offering, which you have given us. I wanted to meet you, you and the other communities, and to tell you that you needn't fear us." She glared at the tall MAG. "Put that away," she snapped.

He holstered the gun but kept his hand on the grip.

"Your Offering is sizable this season, my men tell me." Saige held Amaya aloft and Amaya giggled. "It's too big for such a small community." She smiled at Amaya's mum. "Daisy, is there a Giften in the Field?"

Daisy shrank back, her eyes flicking to the faces of the small crowd.

"Do you need some incentive, my dear?" Saige's voice was low, but still loud enough for me to hear its sickly sweet tone.

Daisy grabbed her arm as she made to climb back into the car with Amaya. The MAGs moved in.

"Stand down!" Saige snapped. Amaya was on her hip now, playing with the long strands of her blonde hair. "Yes?" she said, her head inclined towards Daisy, who swallowed hard, before she leaned in to speak into Saige's ear, her arms outstretched for her baby.

The heads of every adult in the community turned towards Joshie's house.

I didn't understand what was happening, but it had something to do with my friend. Amy's red face, her urgency, Mum telling him to *run*.

As I raced down the porch steps, the MAGs were shoving my friends, my family, aside. One ran ahead to Joshie's cabin, kicking open the door, while the others held the community back with raised weapons. I reached Dad just as Joshie was pushed out of the cabin. Amy hung on to him as the giant MAG started to drag him away. She tripped on the porch steps, got up again, shouting, "*No, please,*" until the butt of a gun cracked against her skull. She went down and stayed down.

"*Joshie!*" I screamed as he was hauled off the ground and dragged towards the solars. All of us were yelling, cursing the MAGs, cursing their guns.

The sky was even pinker now; the Field looked impossibly beautiful in this light; our faces bathed in the glow of a perfect evening.

"You have nothing to be scared of." Saige Corentin's voice cut through our pleas. "I am rebuilding the City. And I have people to feed. Your Offerings and your Giften make that possible."

A MAG appeared at her side, opening the back door of her solar.

"Any Circle here?" she said to him, her eyes sweeping over our faces.

Dad flinched, his grip on my arm suddenly painful.

The MAG shook his head. "We should go, doctor," he said. "We've got everything we need."

The sun glinted off the brooch on her collar, the embossed image of an open palm. "No members of the Circle here? Your revolutionary zeal is disappointing, I have to say." She laughed and climbed into the car. "We will forfeit the next Offering from the Field," she said, before pulling her door shut and disappearing once more behind the black glass.

Joshie, on the backseat of the second solar, struggled with the giant MAG.

When the cars pulled away, Dev started to run after them. I screamed, trying to wrench free from Dad, but he wouldn't let me go.

A MAG leaned out of the window and fired a gun into the sky and Dev stopped dead. His chest heaving, he turned around and screamed his rage into our faces; they had taken his best friend and we had done nothing to stop them.

*   *   *

And then it was dark and I was in bed. Dad loomed over me, arms folded tight across his chest, while Mum cried next door.

"Why did you let them take him?" I whispered. I could barely see him in the gloom. A single yellow candle sputtered on my nightstand, threatening to go out any second.

"I didn't *let them*." His voice broke.

"I didn't know he was Giften."

"No one should have known," he sighed.

We both jumped as the wind thumped against my window. It was black outside, not even the pointy silhouette of the treetops showed against the moonless sky.

I sank back into my bed as Dad shook out my crumpled blanket and covered me.

"It was the food; we gave them too much. It was our own stupid fault; *we* made them suspicious." He was talking to himself now. I thought of the screaming baby—swapped for the Giften boy. "Something needs to change. *We* need to change." He headed for the door.

"Dad," I said, "if we had Circle here, would they have stopped her?" I watched his head fall to his chest. His voice was husky, low.

"Maybe."

PART ONE

The Field

*My hands have worked the land since I was a girl.
Look at them, lined, rough, and calloused. Not much
good for needlework or writing. But they tell my
story just the same. And it's a great yarn, Logan.
It's about raising food to feed the smallies, chopping
wood to keep them warm, holding them close when
they're ill. In this world, you need two things to
survive, one is love and the other is a strong pair
of hands.*

GRACIE, MOORLANDS VALLEY

1

*It's hard to imagine what these lands were once like.
Full of people, full of cars, full of greed. We pumped
out poison and it suffocated us, the land dried to a
crisp or became a sodden wasteland. Whatever they
did to change their ways, it wasn't enough, or it was
too late. Greedy people never really change, they just
find different ways to get what they want. And here
we are, decades and decades after the Darkening,
small communities living in isolated pockets, trying
to feed ourselves off the mistakes of the insatiable.*

FINIAN, INVERS KEEP

Two years ago, Dad and his friend, Owen, went
on a Supply Run, but only Owen came back.

Two long summers have come and gone since
Dad disappeared. Two winters when he wasn't here to
chop up firewood, and two autumns when he didn't
give the Field Day speech. He's missed my fourteenth
and fifteenth birthdays, and I guess I've missed a couple
of his. Some days a careless spark of hope drives me to
glance out of a window, or look up from my chores

outside, thinking I might see him in the distance; he'll be shielding his eyes from the sun, or frowning at the state of our porch steps. Or he'll spy me at my window, wave, yell, *Hello, chicken*.

Mum tried, for a while, to pretend, as the weeks turned into months, that he might find his way back to us, but that was for my sake. It was easier for her to listen to my hopes and wipe away my tears, than to tell me Dad was dead and I would never see him again.

But we saw much more of Owen. He had sat down in Dad's chair at our table that day, saying the same words over and over; they had been ambushed by MAGs, he ran into some woodland, believing Dad was right behind him, but when he stopped running, when he turned around and came out of the woods, Dad was gone.

It feels like Owen took Dad's chair and decided he liked it enough to stay.

*   *   *

Owen and his son, Seb, lived in another community before they joined us; they arrived when I was just a smallie. Their last community had collapsed when the food ran out and Seb's mother had died on the road. I don't remember a time when they weren't here. I once heard Old Pete tell Mum that because Owen was not *born and bred Field stock*, it took him longer to find his place, but hasn't he come to love this land as much as we do? Wasn't it Owen, after all, who had almost single-handedly rebuilt the Shed after the Big Storm five years back?

For a long time, his presence was the black hole into which Dad had disappeared. The single word answers I gave him infuriated Mum, I could tell, and so whenever he came over, she'd send me off to Stace's because she needed to *talk to Owen in peace.* But sometimes I'd just climb back in through my bedroom window and listen. I never heard anything very interesting though, just him apologizing and saying how guilty he felt and Mum telling him it wasn't his fault. That's when I really hated him. He shouldn't be asking her to forgive him. I wished he'd been taken instead.

Finally, I caught something worth hearing. He was saying that he wanted to take care of her, of us, and he wanted to be more than a good friend.

I heard chairs scraping, and then no more words. I opened my bedroom door a crack and peeked. Owen was holding Mum so tight I wanted to scream, his fingers pressing into the soft flesh of her arms, his mouth covering hers, but then Mum's fingers were pulling at Owen's shirt, dragging it over his broad shoulders, exposing his back. And then she caught sight of me. I was no longer hiding, but standing in full view.

Things moved fast after that, and however hard I tried to slow them down, Mum pushed back. *Move on, Ruthie.* Six months later she was pregnant with Ant, and Owen and Seb had moved in. Owen, who had rebuilt the Shed almost single-handedly, wasted no time in adding another room to our cabin for my two new brothers.

But Owen is not my father. And when I tell Mum that he can't be bossing me, or pretending to be Dad, she tells me that he doesn't boss me and he *loved* Dad. Sometimes I see Owen looking at me funny and I know he's wishing I wasn't here, believing that he and Seb and baby Ant are enough for Mum. Stace says that's wrong, that it's sadness in his eyes, not hate, that all he wants is for me to stop blaming him.

There have been fewer Supply Runs since Dad disappeared. Even the MAGs have been stopping by less, we don't seem to get the random invasions that we used to.

Owen's been on pretty much every Supply Run since he joined the Field according to Old Pete, that's how much he cares for the community. He usually takes Seb, now that he's eighteen, or Dev. They bring back the herbs Doc Pam needs for doctoring, salvage for repairing the solars and the cabins, and whatever rusty tools or old books have resurfaced from the days before the Darkening. But now Owen says he doesn't need the company; there are more MAGs out than ever before, why risk more lives? When I asked Mum who put Owen in charge of the Supply Runs, she said he's looking out for us and I should be grateful.

In recent months he's started to patrol the outer perimeter of the Woods, sometimes he's gone for days; she says this is to keep us safe too. But the only people who come uninvited into the Woods are MAGs, and we have no guns to stop them.

*　　　*　　　*

The Field sparkles in the heat today, and the shirts of the men and women harvesting the wheat stick to their backs. Sweat drips off their red faces as they work. Yesterday, when I took my turn with the scythe, a cool wind made the job just about bearable.

In just three months the Field will be under snow. And when you think it can't get any colder, it does, and none of us go outside much, except to check the traps or fetch more wood and food from the Shed. Maybe a bit of hunting if it's clear skies. But right now, at this moment, it's hard to believe in winter at all.

"Hey," I say to Stace. She is sprawled on the dry grass around the Well. Dev, dark skinned with cropped black hair, lies beside her. He's only three years older than us, but he's taller and stronger than most of the men here. Stace squints up at me.

"Hey," she says and shuts her eyes again.

Dev lifts a lazy hand in a wave. Seb sits a little way off, his back against the stone wall of the Well, whittling arrow heads from silver birch to a sharp point.

"Why don't you sit down?" Seb asks, glancing up. It's not midday heat, the sun is already dipping in the sky, but I'm still damp under my thin shirt. His white hair is the opposite of Owen's thick black waves. Owen says his mum had the same colour hair, but Seb was only three when she died on the way to the Field, so he doesn't remember her at all. "I have an extra knife if you want to whittle," he says.

"Too hot," I say.

Stace squints at me again and when I don't move, she sits up slowly.

"What's wrong?" She shields her eyes from the sun.

"I want to talk to you."

Seb and Dev exchange a look. Seb grabs his arrows, shoves them into a pouch, folds away his knife and stands up.

"You don't have to go, we'll go," I say.

"No. It's OK." Seb offers Dev a hand. "We have work to do anyway." They think we're going to talk about bleeding.

"Apple picking?" Dev says, pulling himself to his feet. Seb nods. They head into the Woods, unfolding two sacks for windfall.

"So, what's up?" Stace says, standing up and brushing grass from her skirt. "Let's go to mine. It's too hot out here. Dad's on the roof and Mum's—"

"At mine. I know."

We pass today's harvesters in floppy white hats, stretching and then bending back to it. Old Pete is on his porch making a charcoal drawing on a finely sanded panel of wood; when I follow the direction of his gaze, I see he's staring into the sky. He is drawing from memory.

"Ladies," he nods as we pass.

"Do you think his kids will ever come back?" Stace asks

when we're out of earshot. Old Pete and Lucia's children left the Field when I was a smallie. They wanted to see what else was 'out there', and either they found it and decided it was better than the Field, or they were dead.

"Who knows?" I hope she can tell by my tone that I don't want to get into it.

Stace's cabin is a mess as usual. Bits of wood, tools and salvaged metal are strewn about the main room, the materials her dad, Filip, uses to make toys for the children and fine bows and arrows from yew and furniture from oak for the adults. His wood-turning lathe sits outside in the sun at the foot of the porch, where wood shavings lie in soft blond piles in the grass. Mum is tidy, too tidy Dad thought, and because of her, I guess, I'm also too tidy. I start to stack random blocks of wood and shuffle the tools into a pile, but Stace laughs and knocks the blocks off the table onto the floor.

"Leave it," she says.

I follow her into her room. Her wardrobe hangs open, empty, because her clothes are scattered around her room. Patchwork dresses are draped over the chair, underwear on the floor, trousers on the bed. There is a sort of order to it, I suppose.

We listen for a moment to Filip on the roof, every time he bangs in a nail a shower of fine dust rains down from the beams.

Stace joins me on the bed after flinging trousers on top of dresses.

"So?" she asks.

"Owen found traces of someone camping in the Woods," I tell her.

"What?" She sits up suddenly; her eyes, wide and excited, gaze into mine. "Where?"

"At the Blazes," I say. My voice catches. "Yesterday."

"The Blazes?" she says slowly.

"I know," I say. "He found tire tracks from a solar… and apple cores."

"Shall we go take a look?" She is suddenly on her feet.

I sit up slowly. This isn't going how I planned. "I don't think so. He's telling everyone to stay out of the deep Woods."

I love Stace like a twin, but she isn't one for standing still. She stares at me, her hands on her hips.

"Do you think it's MAGs?" I whisper.

"Of course not!" she says quickly, sitting down on the bed. "Is that what you're worried about, that MAGs—"

"I don't know, Stace," I say, as she reaches for a curl of my hair and twists it between her fingers.

"Come on, Ruthie, let's go see. It's probably someone who just needs help." She takes my hand and pulls me off the bed and over to the window, where she parts the muslins. The sun is setting behind the trees and flashes of red and gold sparkle through the branches. The wind has picked up. I'm glad for the workers. Old Pete chases his hat across the wilting spinach.

"I don't want to," I say. "And Owen said to stay away."

But Stace is already bored of the idea. She's watching Dev and Seb head for the Shed. They each carry a half-filled sack of apples, shoving each other, laughing.

"Who do you think is better looking—Seb or Dev?"

"What?"

"Seb?"

"Seb?" I say, stupidly.

"You like him, don't you, Ruthie?" Stace is staring at me again.

"What? I... Don't be weird, Stace."

"You can't see it, can you?" she says, catching my arm before I can lift the latch on her door to leave. Her blue eyes are large in her face, her voice steady. She really wants to know my answer.

"What's wrong with you?" I say.

"Nothing. I'm an idiot. Just forget it." Her mouth turns down and her eyes glisten.

"Stace? Are you crying?"

"No." She's looking out of the window again. "I'll see you later, OK? And don't worry. It's not MAGs," she says.

*   *   *

Stace and I are the same age, roughly, I'm just ten days older than her. Before we could walk, we crawled all over the Field together, before we could run, we stumbled about in the Woods, hand in hand. I used to think she is the me I'd like to be. Stace is funny and kind; she's also restless. Whenever we've walked up to the outer edges of the Woods, to the strip of land bordering the Field and the outside world, I've caught her gazing at the dusty track the solars take on Supply Runs. She says she wants to see what's *out there*.

This spring Stace and Seb started to go together, and for a while Stace was the happiest she'd ever been, and I thought that maybe one day she and Seb would join and then she'd be my real sort-of sister. But they broke up, and she's miserable. Seb isn't though. Whenever I tried to talk to her about what happened, she just shook her head and looked away. So now I don't bother.

Sometimes I find myself watching Seb when I have no business to. I like the way he blows his snow-white hair out of his eyes on a hot day.

I know what Stace was hinting at, of course I do.

*   *   *

On the way home from Stace's I think about the Field Day celebrations in two days' time. *A moment to pause from all the chores* is the saying. In the Clearing, in the Woods, we share the best of our food and the community takes a day off. Of course, there is the Speech we have to sit through which stings since Dad isn't here to make it. Even though I'd heard him recite the story of the Field every year of my life, something new revealed itself with each telling.

The Speech is partly the story of the Darkening, when our land was once too parched to live off, or drowned by flood water or split by earthquakes. We were broken by the Darkening, cut down by greed, by a lack of care. But Dad's speeches always ended by telling us that something good came out of the ruins—we found *ourselves* again; we, who inherited this broken world, made the Field and the other communities. All we're greedy for now, is life, and having less has made us value our small, everyday victories.

Last year, Owen gave the Speech. He complained about how hard we have to work for so little, how one bad harvest can lead to winter starvation. Maybe we should think about moving further south, towards the Border. He even mentioned my illness and the fever, my *near-death* he called it, and how thankful he was I wasn't *contagious*. Everyone was waiting for him to say that it was all worth it, that living here, in the Field, surviving on the food we grow as a community, is rewarding, but that part never came. Instead of claps and cheers at the end of his speech, there was silence. Old Pete's mouth hung open, Mum looked puzzled and Seb was staring at his own father as if he didn't know him.

"That's bullshit!" Dev was on his feet. "That's not how you give a Field Day speech." He was already taller than Owen. His eyes swept the gathering. "Is it? We're *lucky* here. We feed ourselves. We're doing OK."

"Dev's right," a quiet voice said. Jacintha, Dev's grand-mother. Her white hair was long and loose around her shoulders. "You should know better, Owen."

"And Ruthie was really ill," Dev went on. "We're thankful she's alive, that's what you should be saying instead of all that stuff about being contagious."

Old Pete got slowly to his feet, waving his hands to hush the muttering that had started up.

"It's been tough on all of us since Dan was taken. I'm sure that's what Owen is reacting to." He turned to Owen. "Is that right?"

Owen nodded slowly.

Mum said that Owen is just worried about the future, about the danger to our lives whenever a black solar drives into the Field. About the MAGs.

The MAGs, the men ordered by Saige Corentin to take our food and our Giften.

Before they were MAGs, before they had guns, they were the Rovers; thugs, bullies and thieves who travelled the land in loose gangs, threatening and looting from the communities, but easy enough to resist. And then, more than two decades ago, almost overnight according to Old Pete, Saige crossed the Border from the South to the North. She armed the Rovers and dressed them in black. They became MAGs: Men and Guns—and Giften hunters.

They say the Offerings *and* the Giften feed the people of the City, where the land is rotten, but why should we believe the words of men who kill with an easy twitch of the finger?

But we have no army to fight them.

After Joshie was taken, Dev started to talk about the Circle, how they wanted things to change, how they ambushed MAGs and fought for the communities. But Old Pete and Jacintha and Owen and Mum and nearly everyone else were scared. We weren't fighters. We couldn't risk the little we had.

Owen has asked to give the Speech again this year; Old Pete and the others decided he should have one more chance. Mum says there'll be no surprises this time.

2

The only laws we have are those we make ourselves. In this community, we ration food, we share the work, we punish thieves and no one challenges these rules. I remember a time, when I was a much younger woman, the communities bartered more, shared more, talked more, but the MAGs have put a stop to all that, they've isolated us, made us scared of each other. The rewards for informing on Giften or reporting on the Circle are tempting to those who have very little.

ALICE, CATLAND HILLS

Dad had been gone a year when I got the gift. And just like Joshie, I became a saviour and a danger to the Field. Today, the MAGs would only have to take a walk through the Woods to the patch of burned forest we call the Blazes to know there was another Giften in the Field, someone who could use their hands to raise food from dead earth.

One morning, a month before my fourteenth birthday, I woke up hot and confused. For a few days I'd been watching Mum and Owen; they seemed happy, too happy. A small idea took root and grew; not only had Mum forgotten Dad, but she was *glad* he was gone. She had wanted Owen all along.

On a hot day in July, while the sun punched its way into every inch of the Field and it was impossible to find even a scrap of shade that wasn't suffocating, I shared these thoughts with Stace and Dev.

We were sitting in the Clearing, our backs against the wide trunk of the Giant Oak. Sticky and sweating, I gulped air, incoherent ideas spilling from my mouth; maybe Owen had killed Dad; maybe Mum knew, maybe they had planned it together. The branches of the Oak seemed to be nodding, even though there was no wind. No words came from the stunned mouths of my friends until Stace reached out and touched my forehead.

"You're burning up, Ruthie. We need to get you to Doc Pam."

"You're not making sense, you're ill," Dev said, rising to his feet, holding out a hand to me.

But I ran away from them, deeper into the Woods. I lay on my back by the stream, taking deep breaths; I couldn't get enough air in. The sun broke through the branches and there, in the middle of the light was Dad, speaking softly.

"Ruthie, it's OK. I'm here. I'm right here. Open your eyes."

But my eyes were open. I blinked rapidly. The face hovering over mine wasn't Dad's, but Mum's, and I wasn't in the Woods but at Doc Pam's. I sat up slowly, waving Mum away. My head swam and I fell back onto the cushions of Doc Pam's lumpy sofa.

"Dev brought you straight here," said Mum. "You'd passed out. I need to get you home."

"You've a fever." Owen loomed into view holding out a mug. "Drink some water," he said. I stared into his eyes and saw resentment.

"You drink it!" I shouted, knocking the mug from his hand. Every black hair on his face glinted in the sunshine pouring in through the Doc's kitchen window.

"Let me take you home," he said. His voice was kind, but I could see he was putting it on for Mum. I opened my mouth to tell him I wasn't a fool, when he stepped past Mum and scooped me up off the sofa. By then I had no strength to struggle, so I gave up and lay still as he carried me home to my own bed.

Waking up hot and muddled in the days that followed, my dreams were all about Dad. Mum wasn't in them, or if she was, she was hanging back, standing in the shadows, a giant silhouette beside her. Seb and Stace and Dev were there all the time, sitting by my bed, or standing over me, coaxing me to get better.

And then when I got too ill to even dream, Mum was like the old Mum again. Whether she was stroking sticky, damp hair off my face, or sponging cool well water over my steaming skin, her eyes were full of the old love.

"Ruthie, I'm here. I'm right here," she whispered over and over. Fat tears fell down her cheeks. My fingers itched to catch the drops but it hurt to even raise my arms.

Finally, on one of those hot, hot nights, when the air felt thick and dry, when our small cabin felt more like the inside of the stove than a refuge from the heat, a tingling started at my toes and moved up my body, into my arms and hands. I fell asleep and woke to Mum shouting into my face and shaking me. My body hurt bad. This is how that week passed; deep sleep, thirst, deep sleep and Mum shaking me awake. I don't remember the sky changing from day to night, it was always daytime. I fell asleep in sunshine and woke up in it, washing me in its heat as fast as Mum wiped the sweat from my skin.

Hot sun baked the Field while I baked in my bed. No covers, just sheets that had to be changed so often that Mum gave up and just moved me to the old mattress on the floor till they dried and then moved me back. Stace came every day and just held my hand. She told me funny stories of the Field, the time we thought the chickens had been taken by foxes in the night, but then we found them wandering about the Woods, free of their pen, splashing in the stream. Dev, impossibly tall, sat on my bed and told me that I'd have to work extra hard when I was better to make up for all my chores he had covered.

"Your hair," I whispered. Usually long, hanging in messy waves to his shoulders, it was now cropped close to his head. He looked strange, older.

"Too hot," he sighed. "Have you seen outside?"

He helped me sit up, and pulled aside the muslins at my window. The weight of the heat stooped the shoulders of my friends in the Field as they went about their work. The land was burned yellow, not a single leaf on any tree in the distant Woods twisted in the wind, because there wasn't any wind. It was so still, so beautiful. But that golden glow across the land wasn't beautiful, it meant the crops were going to fail.

It wasn't until the other adults started calling by, that I realized I might be dying. One by one they trooped through my bedroom door, sat for a while, smiling, offering me glimpses of the future; Field Day, rain, exercise. Once the weather broke I would feel better, they promised. Their faces were burned brown from sun and red from the sting of their tears; they had come to say goodbye, to take away a memory of me in that bed, sweating through my pain.

I had believed our small community couldn't afford to lose a worker; I was strong even at thirteen, and gathering enough food for thirty souls was hard, but then, when the smallies came with their mums I changed my mind. Maybe with me *and* Dad gone, this winter wouldn't be as tough as the last.

Mum had to put her ear close to my mouth to hear me whisper this revelation. More than anything I wanted her to know I was ready, that she mustn't be sad for too long. But instead of an understanding smile, her eyes blazed.

Her skin, a deeper bronze from the long summer, blushed red. But facing her anger was better than sitting with her fear. She shouted then, "No! Don't say that!" Not even the strong arms of Owen folding her into a hug seemed to settle her.

On the last day of my illness Old Pete came to sit with me. He has seen the Field grow from a row of shacks into what it is today. But would it have been so different then? The Woods would have still stood tall and strong, sheltering our circle of land. The water still flowed from the Well and the same sun shone down from the sky.

I could barely whisper by then; it was getting harder to swallow and fill my lungs with air. But something about Old Pete was comforting. He had the eyes of a smallie, full wide with wonder and innocent happiness. Grey as it was, he still had his hair, even coming out of his ears. He took my hand in his, his palm was cool, refreshing, leaching just a little of the heat from my skin.

"Now you listen here, Ruthie." He smiled and his face showed a wrinkle for every day he had lived. "I heard you been telling Gemma you're on your way out—a little thing like you. Don't you know you're not allowed to speak that way until your hair's same colour as mine?"

Outside, a burst of starlings swerved over the tallest trees, disappearing on the turn and reforming into a shifting mass before swooping out of sight.

"Shall we take you outside? There's a little breeze today, and you can look at the Woods, see us sweat at our work." He winked a twinkling eye and then I was aloft in Old Pete's arms. Time had taken the black out of his hair but hadn't touched his strength.

Owen stood in the doorway, beside Mum, her teeth gnawing at her lips. I had the thought that Owen might step in, that he wouldn't just stand by and let an old man struggle with my weight, but he didn't. I thought Mum's bump was bigger, and that maybe the baby would fill the gap I left. And then I didn't think about anything; I was outside, struggling to inhale a hot, thick stream of summer.

Stace was at the Well, in the centre of the Field, about to fix the pulley to her bucket. But the moment she saw us, she dropped it and started to run. Seb and Dev emerged from the Woods at the far end of the Field, their arms full of dry wood. In seconds they had dumped the kindling and they too were racing across the land.

I felt Old Pete bobbing down the porch steps, Mum behind us saying, *Be careful* and *Don't trip*, but I couldn't have cared if he did. And then I was in Owen's arms, as he lowered me onto the parched ground and I didn't even have the energy to mind. I felt dry spikes of grass poke through my thin nightie and into my back, my legs. My hands found the grass and I pressed my palms onto the brittle stalks with the little strength I had. And closed my eyes.

Maybe I *was* ready to die now, out here in the Field, surrounded by the Woods, my best friends close. Their low voices were soothing. I felt peaceful and the pain, very slowly, began to ease out of my body. This is what dying is like, I thought, when it's about to happen, you get one exquisite moment of feeling normal again. And then a wild ringing in my fingers.

My eyes shot open as I lifted my hands, but they weren't shaking; they looked normal. Seb and Stace and Dev were on their knees beside me. Finding the ground once more, the grass didn't feel as brittle as it had done moments ago. I closed my fist around a clump, but couldn't pull it out. Either I was too weak or the grass was still alive, despite the heat.

I sat up very slowly, my hands now pressing into softer stalks; I saw that the earth around their stems was darker, almost moist. The pain was ebbing away from everywhere except my stomach.

I was starving.

"I'm hungry," I said.

Seb let out a cry and Stace pulled me into her arms.

"For the love of the land," she said through her tears.

Mum was on her knees staring at me, a hand over her mouth.

A sharp intake of breath from the porch.

Owen was staring at the patches of land where my hands had rested moments earlier.

"We need to get her back inside," said Owen. "Now!"

3

*We ambushed a MAG solar a few weeks ago, on its
way back to the City. Their car was packed with
Offerings. We took the food, the solar, their guns and
their lives. We freed the Giften kids, took them back
to their community later.*

*One of the MAGs, as he lay there, bleeding out,
said a strange thing, "Let me go and I'll help you
become Giften too."*

*I didn't know what to make of it at the time,
but I've been thinking. Is that what's going on at
the Base in the City? They're trying to make Giften?*

IAN, CIRCLE

Within minutes of burying my hands in the
grass, my symptoms had eased. My skin
wasn't on fire and the deep gnawing pain
in my bones was a memory. I could breathe. A different
kind of warmth flowed through me now; it was as though
a terrible thirst had been quenched.

Back in the cabin, I refused to be put back to bed,
demanding food instead.

While Old Pete, Seb, Stace, Dev and I sat at the table, Owen lingered by the door, telling anyone who stopped by that I was feeling much better and would visit with them soon.

"Wow!" Dev said, after I'd polished off a bowl of stew, eggs and most of a loaf of bread. "I guess being Giften makes you hungry."

"I can kill a chicken for you if you like. Maybe two," said Seb.

"Hey, leave the chickens alone." Stace was grinning, her face flushed with relief. "No less than a buck for Ruthie."

Old Pete's smiling eyes followed Mum round the room, as he sipped on the last of Dad's rotting vegetable drink.

"Sit down, Gemma," he said finally. "If we're careful, we can do this."

Mum rounded on him.

"Don't tell me you're losing your mind, old man," she snapped, hands on her hips. No one is rude to Old Pete. "What's care got to do with anything? There is a Giften in the Field. My daughter. And when... and when they come back, if they find out—"

"If, when," said Old Pete. "Come on, Gemma. Slow down."

The anger dimmed in Mum's eyes. Her hands went to her bump.

"Pete, I'm sorry," she said, covering her face with her hands. "Dear God, maybe I'm losing *my* mind." Finally, she sat down. I stared at her, a thick silence hung in the air. And then I ate another slice of bread which Dev had covered with jam. Bright afternoon sun poured through the window, but its heat no longer drained me. I couldn't focus on her fear. I felt numb inside my own head, and had no words.

Old Pete rose slowly. "Gemma, you're right to worry, the rewards for handing over a Giften are real. We've all heard the stories."

The *reward*—a window of freedom from the Offering—for giving up your Giften.

Mum rubbed slow circles onto her lower back as she rose from the table and once again began to pace, her belly straining the seams of her dress.

"She is not to use the gift and that's final," she announced. "We must forget this ever happened."

Owen threw up his hands.

Old Pete downed his cup. "We're not going to sort all this out today. But look at her," he said, and everyone turned to stare at me; I swallowed a mouthful of bread and stared back, stupidly. "We haven't lost her. This is a day of thanks." His eyes brimmed as he stroked my hair, but I was watching Mum as she walked from sink to sofa and back again.

"You know," said Dev, "why should *she* hide? She is one of us, just like Joshie was. They took him and *we* did nothing. If there's something to talk about, it's about protecting our own."

"Don't start all that." It was the first time Owen had spoken since he had carried me inside. "What did you want *us* to do? The MAGs are *armed*, Dev. Where are *our* guns? *Our* army? The Field is not a fortress and we're not soldiers."

"That's not what I'm talking about," said Dev, rubbing a hand over his bristly head. "The Supply Run to Graylings," he was looking at Owen, "you remember, right?"

"I do." Owen glanced at Mum, who had stopped pacing and was frowning at Dev. "There were a couple of Circle there, recruiting for members. But to my mind they're just a bunch of desperate fools who don't have enough to eat, deluding themselves they're heroes. You're young, Dev, easy to see why they might seem special to you, making promises they have no way of keeping."

"Not true," said Dev, shaking his head. "They give us hope. Maybe we don't have to *always* be scared. Maybe we can do something that might give us more control over our lives, over Giften lives. Why have we just accepted Joshie's lost to us?" He was angry. His words washed over me as I remembered Joshie's last day in the Field. The numbness eased and in its place the familiar knot of pain bubbled up in my chest.

"He's not lost," said Seb, defiantly. "He's growing food for the City dwellers."

"You don't know that, Seb!" Dev rounded on him. "That woman took him, took him 'cos he's Giften. You think he's growing food because that's what we've been told to think." Dev folded his arms tight across his chest. "We don't have to believe anything Saige Corentin and the MAGs tell us. We need to find our own truth."

"Is that what you've been doing, Dev?" I exploded. Everyone turned to look at me. Mum squeezed my shoulder. "On the Supply Runs? Talking to the Circle?" The horror of Joshie's ambush was inside me now, painfully fresh. I couldn't lose Dev too. "*Please* don't go off with them."

He knelt beside me, took my hands in both of his.

"Ruthie, if no one ever leaves this place, nothing will change," he insisted. "If we don't—"

"But right now we have to take care of Ruthie." Old Pete's voice broke the spell of my panic and Dev's rage. "And Gemma, you saw how ill Ruthie was? Well, stop her using her gift and she'll get ill again." He winked at me before opening the door. "Ruthie's story doesn't have to be Joshie's, is all I'm saying. We'll find a way to keep her here and let her use her gift, because, if we don't, we've failed another child."

"We keep her gift secret then." Mum was staring at me, like I was a puzzle she was trying to figure out. "No one else must know we have a Giften. Do I have your word?"

Stace, Dev, Seb and Old Pete nodded slowly.

"One plot, then. Deep in the Woods. The Blazes, maybe. We slowly smuggle the food in, and—"

"Not possible," Owen was shaking his head. He stood before us like our leader, his arms folded across his chest.

"Do you really think people won't notice extra food? We have to confess there is a Giften in the Field, but not *who* it is." He looked at me and smiled. "It's a wonderful gift, Ruthie. It could change everything."

But, did he really just say *confess*?

"Let her go to bed," said Seb from the doorway of his room. "We thought she was going to die this morning and now you're talking about putting her to work."

I lay awake that night, thinking about the Giften. What we knew about them mostly came from Logan's stories; the children who can turn a harvest around by burying their hands in the soil. The Giften are rare, Joshie was our first, but even one can save a struggling community.

*   *   *

No one cheered when Old Pete announced there was another Giften in the Field; the memory of Joshie's cries was still too fresh for some. But we had all eaten our fill because of Joshie and that memory was also fresh. While some murmured it was a blessing, others were silent, fearful we'd make the same mistakes.

"We will do this differently," yelled Old Pete over the rumble of voices. "The plots will be hidden. And you will never know the identity of our Giften. And from now on, our Offerings will be small."

"But you know who it is, Pete," yelled Joshie's mum, her face wet with her tears. "Are you ready to sacrifice yourself, or one of us, for this secret Giften?" She glanced at Daisy who was staring at her feet.

She was right. This wasn't a perfect plan and for the first time, shame burned through me. I was risking lives.

But months later, at Turn of the Year celebrations, when our bellies were full, and my gift had raised our meagre stores into more than enough food to get us through the winter, the community was united in silent thanks.

*　　　*　　　*

Thinking about all this puts me in a strange mood as I head home. Today, a year later, the ever-present pulse in my hands is familiar, but I can't get used to the fear, I wear it like an extra garment. Being Giften sets me apart, and I don't like it.

On the steps of our porch I pause for a moment to take in the sky; the sun, a brilliant red, sets into the woodland behind our cabin. I am bathed in pink.

Seb is on his own, making supper. His hair is wet from the shower. He moves around the kitchen as though he has lived here far longer than a single year.

"Hoping it'll rain for Dad's Field Day speech," he says, glancing out of the window as he hands me four bowls, which I set down on the table.

Like Dev, Seb is eighteen, old enough to go on Supply Runs, old enough to start building his own cabin, but he hasn't mentioned it. It's strange to think we both share blood with our half-brother, Ant, but we're not blood family. He hands me four spoons.

"What happened with Stace?" I ask as he stirs something in the pot. He doesn't answer straightaway, but checks potatoes in the oven, and runs his hands through his white hair. Owen's hair is black and Ant, who was no bigger than an ant when he was hatched inside Mum, came out looking more like me, the colour of an apple seed, than his very pale half-brother. He turns to look at me, finally. His shoulders slump and I wish I hadn't opened my mouth.

"We were together, and now… now we're not," he says. His face gives nothing away.

"You can talk to me, you know," I say. "If you want."

"Can I?" His face slackens, something comes into his eyes, a softness. His hands hang limply at his sides, his fingers flexing and unflexing. He looks nervous and suddenly I regret this entire conversation. I'm saved because the front door bangs open and Mum enters with Ant on her hip. My brother has one sticky hand in her hair and the other held out to Owen who follows them inside.

"Food's ready," sighs Seb, turning back to the oven.

"I need to put this kid down," says Mum, yawning. She takes him into her room. We hear Ant's giggles become sobs and then silence. He's as exhausted as Mum.

At supper, Owen announces he's scoured the Woods, that whoever was camped out in the Blazes is gone. The *whoever* is a stranger or strangers. I feel relief first and then a burning curiosity. Why come here at all? Why *there*?

The Blazes, on the distant edges of the Woods, where once a fire ravaged the trees and scorched the earth, is also where Owen created a space for me to use my gift in secret. Over the months, and in secret, I turned this charred land into fertile soil and raised crops with Giften hands.

I shiver to think I was there just a few days ago, with Stace, pulling up carrots, digging for potatoes, filling the baskets for Owen to collect that night and deliver into the community.

"So we're good? Emergency over?" Mum's eyes are red, maybe it wasn't just Ant crying in the bedroom. She slams down her fork and takes a drink of water.

"It wasn't an emergency, Gemma," Owen sighs. "Someone passing through, that's all. A couple of days they'd been there, at most." He wants to move on, but Mum doesn't. And I can't.

"Mum?" I round the table, pull her into a hug. She feels so thin. Worrying about me and taking care of Ant has shrunk her.

"I'm scared, Ruthie," she says softly, meeting my eyes. "Strangers in the Woods…"

I let go of her. She's imagining MAGs sniffing round the Blazes, just like me.

Her fear is a curl of smoke, which I breathe in.

4

*To be old and to have a good memory is a rare thing.
I still remember the stories of my grandmother, who
passed on the stories of her grandparents and their
grandparents. There was a time when one part of
this world could talk to the other, could visit the other.
Moving through the air in a plane, or sailing the seas
in nothing more than a wooden coffin. Impossible to
imagine now; like flying to the moon.*

JACINTHA, THE FIELD

At noon twenty-three adults and nine children gather at the Well before we head into the Woods to celebrate Field Day. The smallies are crazy excited as we begin our walk to the Clearing, and the rest of us are just plain delighted to have a day free from bending over the land.

We move slowly, laden with bags of food, ground mats and a few babes in arms. The sun is high in the sky, a perfect day.

Our ten acres of land, where we grow crops, build our homes and raise the few animals, sits in the middle of this vast forest, on a low hill. I take a last look at the Field before I step into the Woods.

The ten cabins in their familiar semi-circle at the edge of the trees are empty today; there are no smoking chimneys. A ray of sun catches my bedroom window, turning it into a flaming white panel, as though my room is full of blinding white light, a beacon that all is well. Or a warning. A shiver creeps up my spine, everything is so peaceful. So are my friends; Dev, a smallie on his shoulders and another on his hip, Stace and Seb, bags on their backs and hanging from their arms, offering help where they can.

I listen to the easy laughter and realize my Field Day wish is the same as last year; I want to turn back time. Only, it's not exactly the same.

Last Field Day, I longed to have Dad back, but today my wish is to enjoy the day as a non-Giften. I want to go back to the time before I felt afraid. I want to make mud pies with the smallies and weave stalks of dry grass and wildflowers into garlands without fear of the earth reacting to my touch.

We snake down the well-trodden path through this ancient forest which has endured the fallout from the worst our ancestors had to offer. When the weather lost its way, so did parts of this woodland; fresh fire bringing old trees to their knees.

But today sunlight filters through the tall branches of oak and chestnut, through the leaves of the apple, birch and ash. Our feet tangle in the wild bramble and gorse;

flamethrower flowers are collected to adorn our hair. Bees hum a summer song. The mouths of the smallies are already purple with the juice of blackberries. They sing the Field Song with their parents, a marching song of our elders' journey to the Field.

The day passes in a lazy mess of eating, playing, singing the old songs, and finally before the Field Day speech, Dev's grandmother, Jacintha, gathers the smallies and tells them the story of our world. I have heard it many times, even before I could understand words, but it's only in the last few years that I've begun to think about what happened to the world. The oceans taking back the land, the sun burning the goodness out of our food, the measures which failed to hold back the centuries of damage. The wars that split the people as surely as the climate split the earth.

Jacintha paints pictures with her words and her gestures. She spreads her arms wide to take in the Clearing, the Woods, the world. Owen catches her eye, making a circular motion with his finger, signalling for her to wrap it up. He clears his throat and my heart sinks.

"I don't need to tell a single one of you what today means to us," he begins, taking his seat on the trunk of the huge poplar which fell before I was born. The wind has picked up and whooshes through the trees, parting branches so that shafts of thick sunlight fall across our group, illuminating the rapt faces of the smallies. Seb's white hair glows. He isn't looking at his father, but at me. He gestures for me to join him at the edge of the circle.

"Here we go," he says under his breath as I sit down.

"When our world was destroyed," Owen begins, "no thought was given to what might happen to people like us, the survivors." He pauses, bunching his hands into fists. "But we have made a home here. We feed and clothe our young. Our land is fertile." He reaches for Mum's hand. She smiles up at him; Ant is sprawled asleep across her lap.

"We mustn't linger on the past, that would be depressing." Laughter ripples through the community. "We are lucky the MAGs keep their distance, but we must remain alert. We live in a desperate world and our luck could run out." Every adult and older child is sitting straighter now, nodding, agreeing.

A cloud crosses the sun and a gloom settles over our festive day, heat has started to leach out of the Clearing.

"Some people don't understand kindness, generosity, or sharing. So while we celebrate our fortune and hard work, we must have one eye on those who would take it away. We have toiled to make this a safe space—"

"We hear you!" shouts Old Pete to more laughter.

"We will protect what we have, we will cherish what we made, we will never forget the Elders who came before us, who made this possible." Owen puts his hands together and raises his eyes to the tall branches. We all do the same.

I let out a deep breath I didn't realize I was holding. Stace winks at me from the other side of the Clearing; Owen hasn't let us down.

"The land, the trees, the sun," we say. "Thank you."

The wind is up and fat drops of rain snake through the branches into the Clearing. We ignore them, determined to stay outside until dusk. With Stace, Seb and Dev, I walk away from the chatter, the laughter, the squealing smallies, deeper into the Woods. It's quieter now, just the sounds of old trees creaking in the wind, and the woodland stream tumbling over stones. Every Field Day the four of us each tie a knitted cord around a different tree at the edge of the mossy brook. A thank you for their abundance, and their protection. In silence, we pull strips of colour from our pockets and secure them to bare trunks. Around us are all the other trees we have decorated with blue, green, red, pink and orange lengths ever since we were smallies.

"By the time we're old we'll have every tree in the Woods garlanded," says Stace.

"That's if you stay here," teases Dev. I look at Stace; her face is suddenly pinched, pale.

"You're the one who'll leave before me, Dev!" she snaps, turning on him, eyes blazing. I want to tell her to cut it out, not to spoil a good Field day, but it's too late. "You know, it's not wrong to want more than a bowl of food or a smallie in your belly. It's not wrong to want to see what's outside this Field."

"Hey," Dev says softly. "I was kidding. We're all just working it out, you know." He holds up his hands in a peace offering and takes a step towards her. But she holds up a hand and he stops.

"Then stop acting like *I* have to live and die here."

"It's not that simple, though, is it?" Seb's voice is tight. And I have the feeling he's said these very words to her before. "You fling out these words, Stace, but you haven't got a gregious clue. You haven't even been on a Supply Run. All you want to hear from me and Dev is how wonderful it is outside the Field. You don't want to know that it's the same everywhere. Everyone is just trying to stay alive."

Stace's eyes narrow. Her shiny black hair frames her pale face. Freckles meet raindrops on her cheeks. A white streak breaks up the sky.

"I can't go on the Runs because I'm not of age!" Her voice is cold, hard. "And maybe I do want to do more than plant veg and populate the North. Or at least see what's out there before I do. So what?"

Plant veg?

"Hey," I say, but then I let it go. Dev is moving towards her again.

"OK, we get it," he says, laying a hand on her shoulder. She shrugs him off, her eyes fixed on Seb. "I promise I'll take you on your first Run, OK?" A tear or a raindrop runs down her cheek.

And then, suddenly, the three of them become dark shadows; thick cloud has gathered overhead. Lightning splits the sky and the rain comes down. We all look up into the canopy of trees.

"Let's pack it up!" we hear Owen boom.

"Ruthie? Get back here!" calls Mum.

Rumbling thunder chases us back to the Clearing. The wind has come up from nowhere, but now it parts the branches to let the rain in. Everyone is in a frenzy of packing, while the smallies dance in the shower. Stace grabs her baby brother, who is crawling around in fresh mud.

Mum thrusts my squirming, screaming brother into my arms and hoists a bag onto her back. Owen and Filip roll up the ground mats and take down the canvas canopy. I struggle to wrap Ant in a waterproof, but he only wants Mum.

Another crack from the skies and we're off, stumbling through bracken in the rain and wind until we make it to the edge of the Woods, praying it's not like the hurricane from two summers ago which tore the trees in its path right out of the ground.

The Field is no longer green bathed in yellow sunshine. Everything is a dull sodden grey. Branches and leaves and clothes ripped from washing lines carpet the land. The cabins look forlorn, deserted.

"To the Shed!" yells Owen from the back of the straggling, stumbling line. "Storm!" The dread word. How much will we lose? This is the thought running through our minds. How many roofs will leak, how much food will be wasted before it's harvested? The chickens are running a crazy circle inside their pen. Filip and Old Pete shoot ahead to herd them into the shed and their indoor coop.

We cut around the cropland and make for the shelter of the Shed. As the wind whips Ant's hair into my face and the Field is stripped of the last of the summer veg, I think about Stace's words, *Stop acting like I have to live and die here*. Maybe, I think bitterly, if I hadn't been Giften, if I hadn't had to lie to the whole community, if I didn't wake up every morning and for just one moment wonder if today was going to be the day the MAGs snatched me out of the Field, maybe I too might have time to dream about what's *out there*.

Ant has not stopped screaming. His tiny golden face is streaked with rain and tears. "Nearly there, baby," I soothe, but he's having none of it.

The truth is that it has never occurred to me to leave the Field. Stace is desperate to go on a Supply Run, but I'm not. I never have been. Other communities can't be better than ours. I shake the thoughts away; now is not the time.

The rain and wind drive us forward and finally push us through the wide Shed door into a dry and spacious room. Ant instantly goes quiet, awed by the sudden silencing of the storm within these walls. I put him down to crawl.

Once we're all inside and the door has been slammed shut, nervous laughter echoes off the high beams. The chickens pluck and scratch at the seed the smallies launch into their coop. The storm, for it is a storm, rages outside, roaring around the Field, hurling itself against the roof, rattling the heavy beams. The single narrow window shudders.

Faces are red and wet. We towel our heads and replace the children's damp clothing with dry. We joke about *some Field Day*, but I notice Owen is quiet; today will be remembered for the storm, not for his speech.

"We're safe!" Old Pete stands in the centre of the room. He's smiling, his arms spread wide. He turns a slow circle. "We have food, we can ride it out in here if we need to. We're all—"

A sudden blast of wind rips the words from his mouth. The Shed door has been flung wide open, and there, against the gloomy backdrop of driving rain and swirling forest debris, stands a stranger. His eyes are hidden beneath the wide brim of a sandy hat, but he's smiling and—am I dreaming?—impossibly *familiar*. The chatter stops abruptly as every single eye focuses on the bedraggled figure. Even the chickens fall silent.

The stranger steps into the room and kicks the door shut behind him. His wet shirt clings to his bony frame, his hat drips rainwater. He pulls it off and smiles. His black beard is longer than Owen's, curlier. He has the same apple-seed skin as mine. Scanning the room, his eyes come to rest on my face. With a husky voice, he says my name. My fingers itch and fizz. The ground tilts. Someone—Seb?—is suddenly beside me, catching my arm as I stumble.

I'm aware of the wind crashing against the walls, debris from the Woods hitting the roof. The world inside this space holds its breath, but outside it is screaming.

My head fills with a low hum. I look into the stranger's face. I'm aware he's been talking to me all this time.

The stranger is my dad.

"You're not dead," I say, numbly.

"I'm very much alive," Dad says, his face collapsing, before he pulls me into his wet arms.

5

*The MAGs run everything from their big house in the
City, the Base they call it. Only it's not a home, is it?
Who knows why the Giften never come back? Don't tell
me it's because those wee scraps are happy in the City.
If you ever find out, make sure you write it all down.*

MORRIS, NARROW KEEP

I can hear his heart beating in his chest. I smell rain
on his shirt and something else that's more like a
memory than an aroma—it's Dad's unique scent,
made up of everything he's ever meant to me. I am inside
a perfect moment.

I become aware of the other voices, excited, wildly
curious. They have only one question, *Where have you
been?* He lets me go and others move in. I stare and stare
and stare. Dad is back. Dad isn't *dead*.

The faces of the community show more than curiosity
and joy at his return. I sense fear; they're scared by the
hungry look in his eyes, the scars of old cuts and scrapes
to his gaunt face. His new beard. Is he still Dan? I turn
around to look for Mum, but see Owen instead.

He's standing to one side as a huddle forms around my missing father, his eyes flicking between Mum who is staring at Dad open-mouthed, and Dad.

But now Dad is looking at Mum too, and the crowd parts as she walks into his open arms, Ant on her hip. She moves slowly, as though she's having to concentrate on putting one foot in front of the other. She's saying words which none of us can hear into his ear. He's nodding slowly, his eyes on the far wall of the Shed and his arms tight around my mum and her son.

Candles have been lit against the dim light and now it throws their image onto the Shed wall, a huge silhouette of the wrong family.

I watch Dad take in Ant's golden skin; he touches his soft round cheeks. The adults turn their heads, start to talk amongst themselves; this scene too intimate to witness.

"Ruthie, are you OK?" Dev whispers into my ear, startling me back into the room. Stace circles an arm around my waist.

"It's really him, isn't it?" I whisper.

"It is." A catch in Stace's voice.

"I speak for everyone," announces Old Pete. "Where, for the love of the land, have you been, Dan?"

Lucia hands Dad a large slice of honey cake in a square of yellow cloth. Filip gives him a steaming mug. Dad stares at both, as if he doesn't know what they are, or what to do with them. And then he takes a large bite of cake and chews. A gust of wind hammers the door and he startles, spilling hot tea from his mug. His eyes are on the door.

"Just the wind," says Old Pete.

"Sorry," Dad says. "Just jumpy."

"Come on, Dan," says Stace. She is desperate to hear his story. Everyone is. But right now, all I want is to be alone with him and Mum. It's a powerful urge. I want to go back to our cabin; just the three of us. I want to shut the door and make tea and sit at the old table and watch the sun set from the kitchen window. I want Mum to want the same thing, but she's not even looking at Dad any more, she's watching me.

"Owen told you about the MAG ambush, you know that much, I guess," Dad begins, locking eyes with Owen. "I was taken to the City, to the Base, and that's where they kept me for a year."

"In a cell? A prisoner?" asks Filip.

Dad has to raise his voice against the wind battering the Shed. He nods. "I escaped." A chorus of gasps.

"Thank God!" says Dev, and then, "How?"

Jacintha, his grandmother, nudges him. "He wants to fight the MAGs," she says, laughing.

"I hear you, Dev," says Dad. "All in good time." Dad nods at Owen. "I'm glad you escaped, friend. If we had tried to fight them together we would have both died."

Owen shakes his head slowly. "I didn't *escape*, Dan." His big voice is loud, but not angry. "I ran. And I thought you were behind me. Right behind me."

"Well, whatever you did, it saved us both." Dad grins, but it's not funny.

"But you weren't saved!" I explode, finding my voice at last. "He was taken prisoner. He's been gone for two years!" I shout into the faces of my friends and family. "This isn't a gregious campfire story!" Stace tries to take my arm, but I shake her off. "You all thought he was dead, even *you*, Mum. But *I* didn't, I—"

"It's time," Dad cuts me off, "to tell you who I am." He isn't grinning any longer. He drains his tea and wipes his mouth with his wet shirt sleeve.

Beyond him, outside the small window, I see a heavy grey sky; it's almost dark even though it's only late afternoon. Debris spins in small circles around the Field; sticks and toys and leaves fly through the air. I flex my fingers; I would like to bury my hands in the mud right now.

*   *   *

"Dan is amazing," whispers Dev, as Dad tells the story of his escape; a snatched key in the dead of night, a fight and then flight.

"The MAGs take our food and steal our children." Dad sounds like he's giving a speech. His eyes shine. "But they are not unstoppable." He pauses, he surveys the room. "A long time ago I began to use the Supply Runs to reach out to the other communities, to encourage resistance to the MAGs, to Saige Corentin's hold over us and our land. But I was betrayed."

A cold hand clamps around my heart. For a crazy moment I wonder if I've got it wrong, that this stranger isn't Dad after all.

"Resistance starts with raised voices, and maybe my voice was too loud," he says. "The MAGs had their eye on me. But this fight doesn't stop with me. Even if I'm dead."

"I'm in!" shouts Dev. He's found his hero, but I feel sick. Dad is prepared to die for *this fight*.

"Dev," Dad laughs. "You're so tall." He moves towards Dev and draws him into a hug, but then he pulls away and turns back to expectant faces. We're all waiting for him to continue. "I'm talking about the Circle, and we're gathering strength. This is our land and in my small way I am helping to build another voice which might one day become as loud as the MAGs." But no one cheers. No one was ready for this. Dan is back, but he's still a stranger.

Distant thunder rumbles in the sky. The clouds and rain and the wind have left the Field. The Shed is too warm; those still in damp clothes are beginning to steam. The final few rays from the setting sun find their way through the small window and seem drawn to Dad's face, picking out the lines on his forehead, the grey flecks in his beard. But there is a special light in his eyes, and the light is also a feeling, the same feeling I get when I plunge my hands deep into dry, dead soil and burrow down, to find moisture; it is the light of hope.

Maybe I'm not that surprised to find out that Dad is part of a resistance.

I watch him joke with Old Pete, but very soon I will extinguish his happiness with a few simple words. I will tell him something that will scare him just as much as the MAGs. Because that's what I do. I put lives in danger. Old Pete catches my eye. His sad smile tells me he knows what I'm thinking.

*   *   *

Just hours ago we were picnicking in the sunshine and now twenty-three adults and nine children head for home. The ground is littered with woodland debris, clothing whipped from washing lines, thick branches, a billion leaves, damp pages ripped from precious old books, sodden, disintegrating and now lost for ever. I pretend I'm picking up a few items, and push my fingers deep into the wet earth at the edge of a beaten-down veg patch and hold them there, feeling the familiar warmth spread up my arms and into my body. I wipe my hands clean on the grass. Dad lingers, waiting for me, his gaze is fixed on our cabin. When the tension in my hands has eased I join him, holding damp pages and someone's muddy skirt.

"I thought about you every day," Dad tells me. "Just the idea of you, happy and healthy, gave me enough strength to find my way home."

Home, I thought, how could this be his home when another man was now Mum's One and Only?

We fall into silence as we approach the Cabin. Everyone else is inside. Dev and Stace wanted to come back with me, but I told them I had to see this through alone. Dev thinks I shouldn't tell Dad just yet, let him settle back into life in the Field, but I want to, right here on the porch steps. I even catch his arm as he starts to climb, open my mouth to say the words Mum is so scared of. But when he turns around, the look of hope has gone. This isn't his house any more. Mum isn't his One and his little girl is older, too serious, a hesitancy in her joy at his return. I can't do it.

"It's going to be OK, Dad," I say instead.

6

The MAGs went straight for Michelle; they knew she was Giften. Someone had given her up and our reward was freedom from the Offering, for a while at least. When we found out who it was we put him out. A bitter old man who wouldn't ever eat Michelle's food, insisted on growing his own, never one to share. He was scared of her. Thought her gift was unnatural.

VICTORIA, LEAFY GROVE

I n the centre of our family room sits the table Dad made with Filip when I was a smallie. Now I watch him run his fingers over the worn grooves that spell out our names on its surface.

The same rag rugs cover the rough boards, and the wood-burning stove tucked into a corner of the room will soon roar with fire just as it did two years ago. Against the back wall a couch of lumpy cushions, too uncomfortable to sit on, is the only other furniture. Owen wanted to get rid of it when he moved in, but Mum said the day the couch goes he goes with it.

"This can't wait, Gemma." Dad doesn't sit down, but leans over the table, arms tense, palms spread, while Mum and Owen strip off damp layers. They don't look at him and I hate them for it. Seb takes Ant into his room to change his nappy. "I need to talk to you. Both of you."

Owen fills the kettle and starts the fire in the cook stove. For an insane moment I think Dad's going to tell them Owen should move out. That this is *his* home. *His* One.

"The Field is in danger. You are *all* in danger," he says instead.

They turn around then, slowly, reluctantly. The tingling starts in my fingers and I rub my hands together. Mum shoots me a look. *Stop it*, her eyes say.

"I know what's going on here and you're fools if you think you're safe." Dad pounds one hand on the table.

Mum's mouth is a thin line. She sits down. The kettle whistles.

"What are you talking about?" Owen says. "What danger?"

Ant crawls out of Seb's room, gurgling nonsense. Dad's old chair, made by Filip before I was born, creaks as he finally takes a seat, laying his dry and calloused hands flat on the table. Mum watches him in silence.

"You know exactly what I'm talking about," he says. Owen hands him a steaming mug. "The *Blazes* of all places? Someone has been growing *outstanding* plots of fresh food in charred earth. What exactly do you think will happen when the MAGs find them, Gemma?" Mum

71

opens her mouth, but nothing comes out. Dad hasn't finished anyway. "They will torture each and every one of you until you hand over the Giften." Beads of sweat pop on his forehead. I fidget in my chair. I'm too hot. I shiver. Too cold. The pressure in my hands builds and I clench them into fists.

A picture of Joshie flashes in my mind; beaten and bloody.

The colour slowly drains out of Mum's face.

"*You* were camping at the Blazes?" I ask, confused. He nods, his eyes still on Mum.

"I meant to come straight here, but…" He shakes his head slowly, no longer angry, but sad. "I needed a couple of days. I knew about you and… and Owen. I thought I was OK. Hell, I even understood, but when it came to it…" Dad shrugs. "I *can* help, Gemma. I can take the Giften to safety, I can—"

"No one is leaving the Field." Mum finds her voice at last. "This is none of your business." She glances at me, just once, very fast. Another warning shot to keep my mouth shut.

"It is my business!" Dad is on his feet again. "Thank God I came back before… before—"

"Mum," I say, before I knew I was going to say anything at all. "I think—"

"Stay out of this, Ruthie!" Mum snaps. "Go to Stace's, or Dev's. Right now."

"Dad," I say, swallowing the hard lump in my throat.

"Ruthie!" She's on her feet, moving round the table. "Please!"

"It's me, Dad," I say. "I'm the Giften." Mum stops dead, her hands cover her face, head down. She lets out a low moan.

The words I have been forbidden to speak for so long felt strange in my mouth. Dad's eyes search my face, as though he hasn't understood me, as though the sense of what I've said is written on my cheeks or on my chin.

And then he turns away from me and vomits. Silence in the room. Even Ant isn't moving, he stares up at me, understanding I have unleashed a forbidden truth into the room.

Through the window I watch the clouds part in the dark sky to reveal a full moon. Hovering over the dark silhouette of the trees, a moonbow appears, shimmering and misty and so beautiful. I hold my breath. Dad is bent double, heaving. Mum leans heavily on the table, her eyes shut. Owen tries to take her arm but she swats him away.

"I'm sorry," I say, once Dad is upright, wiping his mouth with his sleeve. The yearning to tell him has vanished, but something else has taken its place. Regret.

Seb passes Dad his tea which he gulps down.

"It's OK, Ruthie. It's going to be OK," he whispers.

"Didn't you hear me?" Mum says. "The Giften is *not* leaving the Field. Especially when that Giften is *my* daughter. If you want to protect her then stay here and protect her." Mum and Dad stand at either end of the kitchen table. She's breathing fast, as if she's been running.

I can't help thinking how beautiful Mum looks right now and for an insane moment I wonder if Dad's thinking the same thing. Her cheeks are flushed, her hair a crazy mess of black curls. Green eyes that would shoot fire if they could.

"I can't stay here," he says quietly. "It's not my home any more. You know that, Gemma."

"So you came back for what? Just to say hello? All this talk about the Circle. You're trying to start a war! And you're crazy to think I'd let you drag Ruthie into your fight."

"So what's your plan then, Gemma? Just take your chances, cross your fingers? Hope no one notices?" Dad points at Ant who sits on the floor, grinning up at him. "A MAG finds the plots, grabs a kid—let's say *this* kid—how long before Owen gives up Ruthie for his son?"

Owen suddenly comes to life. He steps up to the table and jabs a finger at Dad.

"Don't try and second-guess me, Dan," he says. "Ruthie is Ant's sister, for God's sake. She's Gemma's daughter. She's part of this family and I can take care of her." For a moment I feel a rush of warmth towards him. But then he sighs, rubbing his beard, glancing at Mum. "But maybe Dan has a point, Gemma. He *is* her father, he—"

"Dad! For the love of the land!" bursts out Seb. "What are you saying? That he should take Ruthie?" Seb is staring at his father open-mouthed.

"Of course not! I'm saying let's listen to the man."

My mouth drops open too, as Mum slaps Owen hard across the face. His head snaps back and Ant starts to cry.

"Gemma!" Dad barks, but she doesn't seem to hear him until he says, in a softer voice, "You could come with us."

Owen's face fills with colour. He jabs another finger at Dad.

"Ruthie's your daughter, fair enough, but Gemma is *my* One now," he booms.

Mum turns to him, her voice is flat.

"I don't belong to you, Owen, and neither is Ruthie yours to give away."

"I didn't mean she should go." Owen is suddenly desperate. "Just that we should listen—"

"This has nothing to do with you. Nothing." There is a dangerous edge to her voice now. For a long time no one speaks.

"They're collecting Giften in the City," Dad says finally, into the silence. "And it's not to grow crops. I was there, I heard things. They're experimenting on them."

Mum seems to deflate. She grabs the edge of the table for support.

"Experiments?" My voice is thick, strange in my ears. "What experiments?"

There is a pot on a shelf beside me. This morning I threw some loose soil into it to see what would grow. The urge to bury my hands in its contents is too strong to resist.

Absentmindedly, I stir the earth with my fingers. Tiny white shoots reveal themselves just beneath the surface. If I could just focus on the soil maybe all this would go away.

"Saige Corentin has some crazy ideas. She thinks the gift can be passed on. That normal people," he catches my eye, and winces, "sorry, that non-Giften can become Giften. And people are dying while she tries to prove it."

The pot slips from my hands and smashes, scattering ceramic fragments and tiny shoots all over the floor. How can the gift be *taken*? What has she done to Joshie?

Outside, the Field is bathed in moonlight. For a moment I think about the work we will have to do in the morning. I think about the windfall to be collected and the paths to be cleared, about the ruined end of season veg and what might be salvaged. I think about my plots in the Woods; will they be OK? I think about leaving the Field. The thought startles me back into the room.

"You were gone for two years, Dan, but only imprisoned for one, is that right?" Mum is speaking slowly. "If you cared so much about Ruthie, why didn't you come straight back here?" She moves to the stove, and pours hot water over dried mint leaves.

Dad sighs and interlacing his fingers he rests his hands on the top of his head, a familiar gesture that tugs at my memories and my heart.

"I found out about you and Owen. A year ago." His voice breaks as he meets my eyes. "I'm sorry, chicken. I needed time. I lost so much in that place, and then I lost your mum. So I just carried on, moving around, talking to people about a different future." He sighs again. "What I want to say is that, in the end, the desire to see you, Ruthie, was too strong, so here I am."

"But you're not staying, are you? And now you think you can take Ruthie with you." Mum chucks her tea down the sink.

"She's our daughter, but right now," he tells her, "I'm the parent who seems to care whether she lives or dies." He looks at Owen. "And you," he says, "you have to know by now that Gemma only does what she wants. I could no more make her come with me than I could make you." Dad turns to me and smiles sadly. He heads for the door, but I catch his arm.

"Where are you going?" I'm suddenly convinced that if he leaves now I won't ever see him again. He takes my hand and presses it to his chest.

"I'm sorry, chicken. I can't stay here. I'll be at the Doc's."

*   *   *

Long ago when Doc Pam was known as Young Doc Pam, when she first took the purple sash of the medic, she made a gong from salvage. It's big and round and hangs over the Well. When it's walloped with the wooden mallet the sound vibrates through your bones. Even deep in the Woods it will call you home. If someone is hurt, or a storm is coming, or a new baby is born, we come running when we hear the gong.

I am woken very early the next morning by its thick, thunderous clangs. A surge of panic races through me as I push the muslins aside to reveal weak sunlight, and Dad—lifting the heavy mallet and striking the surface of the gong, over and over.

Between the fizzing in my fingers and the buzzing in my head I struggle to get my clothes on. Stepping out onto the porch I see Mum and Owen and Seb approach the Well along with everyone else in the Field. I force myself to run and when I reach them I grab Mum's arm. She looks at me with wild eyes.

"I'm sorry to wake you so early," shouts Dad. "Especially after the events of yesterday." His eyes sweep over the expectant faces of the community, young and old. And then he finds me and holds out a beckoning hand.

I push past Mum, past Seb and Stace and Dev until I'm by his side.

"Dad," I pant. "What are you doing?"

He lowers his mouth to my ear. "This is the only way, chicken," he says softly. "Will you trust me? Do you remember enough of me to trust me?"

I look into his eyes. They're on fire.

I nod, somehow knowing this moment will change everything. He takes my hand and holds it over his heart, just as he did last night.

"Time is not on my side and I have something to tell you," he booms. "My beautiful daughter…"

Everyone is staring at me.

"No!" Mum screams, launching herself through the crowd, but she's too late, the words are out of his mouth.

"… is the Giften."

Mum is clawing at him. He pushes me aside and grabs her wrists until she stops fighting and collapses, sobbing against his chest. He doesn't let go, and she doesn't pull away. Even though she's the one who is crying and Dad is the one who has just changed our lives for ever, every eye is still focused on me.

Dev, appearing from nowhere, wraps strong arms around me, shielding me.

"It's OK, Ruthie. It's OK," Stace whispers as she too draws close.

"Gemma. Everyone knows now," Dad is saying. "Everyone. Ruthie has to leave. I found her plots easy enough, it wouldn't take much for the MAGs to do the same." Stony faces stare back at him; the joy at his return has already vanished. "There are rewards for handing over the Giften, threats to our lives if we don't, and none of us is invincible."

*   *   *

It had happened slowly. I began to notice I didn't laugh as hard at my friends' jokes, or join in their games or run as freely through these Woods as I used to. The company of more than four or five adults made me nervous. Becoming Giften meant our bellies were fed, that we had better rations in the cold months. But the ever-present seed of fear had started to grow inside me the second my hands touched the brittle grass in my fever. We were all in danger because of me.

Dad is here to deliver the Field from danger. But it means I must leave my home.

7

You've heard the stories about the Sanctuary; the wild Giften who would kill you with an arrow as soon as say hello. Those stories are true enough, but only if you're in the business of killing them. We met a couple once, and that's how I know. They came by the community to take a Giften child to safety; we had no choice, the MAGs were long overdue a visit and the land was a holy miracle of food. Two women—twins they were—didn't speak much to anyone but the girl. They were kind. Truth is the Sanctuary spreads these rumours to keep the MAGs afraid. I've seen more savagery in the chicken coop.

EDDIE, CUMBERLANDS

he sky is a rare colour today, patches of pale lilac gather and fade. By mid-morning a sea of white cloud hovers over the Field. It's cool after the storm. From my bedroom window, I watch my friends bend to the task of clearing the land, even the smallies.

I climb out of Seb's window, which backs onto the Woods, and slip into the forest's shadows. Half an hour later I'm deep inside. The birdsong is rowdy; almost painful to my ears. My eyes are gritty from lack of sleep. Two crossbills fly with me for a while, the exact colours of autumn. They call out to each other, back and forth, and fly off when I reach my destination—the Blazes, where once, a long time ago, a great fire raged. Nothing grew here until I put my hands into the ashy earth. For a year I have tended this scorched ground; digging the soil, planting seeds.

Now, my fingers tingle with anticipation, but it's more than that, it's my entire body that feels the connection. Old Pete said I have a *symbiotic* relationship with the earth; the soil needs me to thrive and vice versa. But today it feels like I'm saying goodbye to the thick leaves of spinach, the black-eyed peas, the bulbous squash and the dense brown soil.

Yesterday, I was going to live here till I died.

For a few seconds, after Dad's words changed my life, the only sound in the Field was the gong's vibration. Joshie's mum, Amy, wouldn't look at me and neither would baby Amaya's mum, Daisy.

"Let her go, Gemma," Amy said, her face twisted with regret and longing. "I wish Joshie had had that option. Keep your child safe because if you don't, she'll be murdered or worse." And now I knew what *worse* was. It was being experimented upon by Saige Corentin. With those words, she turned on her heel and headed home.

Dev had more to say, insisting this was my home, that we should arm ourselves, challenge the MAGs, ask the

Circle for help, while others agreed that it would be best to get me away to safety, and not just for my sake, but for theirs. Lucia thought the Field needed my gift if we were to thrive, that I couldn't just be cast out, that we weren't stupid, we would find a way. We had learned our lesson. She reminded us of the many winters when we had come so close to the end of our stores. One by one they had their say. Never had we been so divided.

*   *   *

"Ruthie?" Lost in these thoughts, my hands buried up to my elbows in thick, moist dirt, I startle. The earth beneath my fingers pulses, pushes, as though it's trying to get under my skin.

"Hello, Seb," I sigh. I have no more words left.

"Ruthie. I… I wanted to talk to you." He stares into my lap; at the small orange pumpkin I had just plucked. "It's too crazy back there. Your mum… Gemma's really upset." He joins me on the ground as I lift my caked hands out of the earth. He looks tired. There are purple patches under his eyes.

"I want to come with you," he says, simply. But these are not simple words. They confirm I'm leaving my home, the Field, everyone I love.

"Come where?" I snap, as he reaches for my muddy hand and squeezes. He lifts it to his lips. "Don't!" I snatch my hand away. He looks at me for a long moment.

"Ruthie, you have to know how I feel about you," he says slowly. "You can't—"

I'm on my feet in a second, the pumpkin tumbling to the ground. I take a step back.

He rises slowly, moving towards me. "I've tried to tell you. And now... now you might be *leaving*." His green eyes bore into mine.

"Stace is my *friend*, Seb. How can you say... say all that? You're supposed to be my *brother*." The rage building up inside me has little to do with Seb or Stace, but it feels so good to be angry. It's better than the feeling of numb speechlessness ever since Dad told everyone I was the Giften.

"I don't want to talk about Stace and I'm not your brother. I can't lose you."

I hear his words, and maybe I would have liked them better three days ago, maybe not. But right now, they sound like another problem I don't need.

"Lose me?" I say. "You don't have me." His expression goes from sad to serious. "Weren't you there when Dad told everyone I have to leave? Did you hear Amy tell me to go or be killed? Or... or worse?" He has no idea what it's like to be *me*. "Even Owen thinks I'm putting the Field in danger. You had someone who loved you. Stace loved you, and I don't have space in my head for whatever this is." I wave a hand between us.

He sighs and looks away. "She wants more than the Field. More than I could ever give her. She thinks there's something better out there, a different life; she's the same as Dev. And… and I love that about her, I do. But then she starts making plans and suddenly, I was a part of those plans and then… and then… Well, I didn't want to be with her any more." The words spill out of his mouth. "Is that what you wanted to hear, Ruthie?" He moves closer, eyes flashing. "That your best friend doesn't give a stuff about the Field and can't wait to leave?"

"That's not true. She's… she's just different." I stare at my boots.

"She thinks you're *lucky* to be getting out."

"Lucky?" I whisper. "You've got no idea. Maybe she wants to get out, visit some communities, maybe even the City, but she's my best friend, and just like the rest of you, if she feels anything for me, it's pity."

*   *   *

When I get back to the Field I join everyone else to work on the land until the early evening sky is a grey blue shot with a fiery red, and the trees become a dark mass, shifting slowly in the wind. Smoke pours from the chimneys, in white clouds, moving with the wind until it disperses. The land has been cleared, and the vegetable patches picked bare. It's too late in the season to start planting fresh seed, so we will have to make the best of what we can save. We. But that's wrong, *they* will have to make the best of it.

No one spoke to me much as we worked side by side, but they touched my shoulder as they passed, squeezed my hand, until I couldn't stand it any longer and headed for home.

Dinner is eaten in silence. Mum moves food around her plate, but doesn't eat. Seb hasn't come home at all. Without asking for permission, I tell the room I'm going to see Dad. At the Doc's.

"No, Ruthie." Owen shuffles to his feet and carries his empty plate to the sink. "There's a community meeting, in the Shed," he says. "We're all going."

And then I'm on my feet too. Mum doesn't move or say a word, staring numbly at her untouched food.

"Mum! Owen can't stop me seeing Dad. He—"

"It's Dan who called the meeting," Owen cuts in. He moves his big body so he's in front of the window, blocking out the pinky sky. Ant is awake, baby noises coming from Seb's room, and Mum leaves the table to fetch him.

"My dad?" When Mum comes back into the room, Ant is strapped to her front, in his sling, asleep once more.

"Ruthie, I need you to listen to me," she says, laying her hands on my shoulders. "I can't stop this happening. I wish I could, I've even wished Dan had died before he could come back and take you away from me. But now... now that we've... I've had some time to think." She glances at Owen. "If you went for a while maybe we could find a way to bring you back safely. Or maybe we could all leave the Field, go somewhere where no one knows that you're..." She drifts off.

"*Where* is Dad taking me?" I yell. I was wrong to trust him. "*Where* is this magic MAG-free Giften paradise?" And then in a flash it comes to me. Of course. I shiver.

"No," I whisper.

Mum is watching Owen, but he's looking at me.

"Dan says it's not what we think it is, Ruthie, it's—" he begins.

"The *Sanctuary*? You're talking about the Sanctuary?" My face feels hot. I take Mum's hands from my shoulders and drop them. "You knew about this?" I ask her.

Owen opens his mouth again, but I hold up a hand. "I'm asking *her*!"

Mum meets my eyes. She looks so sad that for a moment, an instant, I want to tell her it's OK, I'll be fine. She mustn't worry.

"Dan believes you'll be safe with them," she says softly. "For now."

8

We were on a Supply Run when they stopped us. I knew straight away they weren't no normal community folk with all the bows on their backs, knives in their belts. I was so scared I near wet myself, but then one of them, a woman—strong she was, hair in thick ropes—told me their solar had broken down and they needed help; she meant us no harm. We did what we could, got the car going, and they gave us food and even a drop of wine. Just before they set off, the woman stuck her head out of the window and told us we were lucky to escape with our lives and they all burst out laughing. Sanctuary they were, I'm sure of it. Wasn't much savage about them at all.

BERNIE, PENTLAND DOWNS

The moon is out and apart from the odd flurry of animal life in the treetops and owls hooting to their babies that they'll return soon with food, the night is still. It's hard to believe the storm happened at all. It's getting dark fast; the trees become a single vast cloud of black.

The same candles which welcomed Dad home a couple of nights ago cast a flickering yellow light over the faces of everyone in the Shed. The smallies aren't here though. The rage I felt just moments earlier is gone. My mind floats in the wooden rafters of the ceiling, as plans are hatched for my future.

Sacks of onions and potatoes line the back wall, our dusty farm tools along another. Broken furniture sits in one corner, waiting for Filip's time and attention. Flour swirls around the grinding stones whenever the door is opened. From the indoor coop, the chickens cluck and jump with annoyance at this sudden bedtime interruption; their feathers fly.

Stace takes my arm, leading me away from Mum and Owen.

"Ruthie," she whispers. "What's this about?" I shake my head and don't say anything. A cold lump sits in my throat.

I see Dev, a head taller than anyone else in the room. He waves. Seb sits atop a sack of lumpy veg, watching me.

"He's sulking," says Stace. "I've tried to talk to him." She's sad again, but I feel selfish.

"What's he got to sulk about?" I say meanly. "He's not the one who has to go and live with the Sanctuary."

Stace takes a step back, a hand over her mouth. Old Pete and Lucia, Filip and Doc Pam; all of them are smiling at me, pityingly. My eyes fill with baby tears, and I rub them away with my sleeve. The horror in Stace's face turns to sympathy and I want to slap her.

Dad, in the centre of the room, clears his throat and holds up his hands for silence. Mum moves through the crowd to stand by his side but Owen stays back. They are united at last, my parents. It was a journey, but they got there. All it took was my *gift*, this great power to raise food from the land. And it will send me into the jaws of a nomadic community who hate the non-Giften.

"Ruthie and I will be leaving before the MAGs come for the harvest Offering," Dad announces. People mumble and mutter. He places his hand over his heart. "No harm will come to her, I promise you. And when it's safe I will bring her back."

Questions are fired at him. *Where is he taking me? When will it be safe?*

"Please. Everyone," Dad calls out and the voices fall silent. "I'm taking her to the Sanctuary." The voices rise again, louder this time. "Whatever you've heard about them is not true. I believed the rumours and then I met them."

"Dan, come on," calls Filip. "They're *nomads*. Ruthie is a child."

"I have helped many Giften to safety. Many *children*. The Sanctuary feeds the stories, Filip. Would you approach them? Would I? No way. But then, one day, I did."

"But they're... they're killers." Stace is pale; I wonder if she's still jealous of my wonderful adventure.

"We're all killers," says Dad, his voice rising. Gasps echo around the room at his words. "When we have to be. They take care of their own. That's what matters."

"How do we get her back?" Dev looks very young suddenly, like the boy who chased after Joshie all those years ago.

"The Sanctuary isn't a prison, Dev, and it's not another country. Ruthie is free, they're all free," Dad tells the room. "But some choose to stay and do whatever they can to keep the Giften safe from the MAGs."

"Dan wants a volunteer to go with him," calls Mum and from Dad's face I can tell this is *her* idea. Her voice is clear, louder than Dad's. Ant gives a whimper and she strokes his head. "You will go to the Coast, meet with the Sanctuary and when you're *both* absolutely sure she will be safe, Dan will bring you back." She smiles, as if she's just issued an invitation to an adventure in the Woods.

"I'm going!" Dev steps forward. "Of course I'm going." He's grinning at me, but I don't smile back. I don't want to be here.

"I can't be responsible for other people's children," Dad says, sighing. "I'm sorry, Dev."

And then an odd sound; Jacintha, Dev's tiny grandmother, is laughing.

"Oh Dan, you've been away too long. Does he look like a child to you?"

All eyes on Dev now, he flexes his lean muscly arms. His cropped hair has given him a hungry look. *And* he's so tall. Dev turns a slow circle.

"That's right," he says. "Eyes on me."

"Seb will come with you, too," a voice booms out. "Three are better than two," says Owen and Seb jumps off the sack of onions and goes to stand beside Dev. He is the opposite of Dev, his skin although a little tanned from the sun is still very white next to his friend's nut brown. Seb's hair catches the candlelight and glows a pale yellow. The boys slap hands in the air and my heart catches. I hear a small gasp beside me; I turn to see Stace walking away.

"Thank you, Seb," says Mum before Dad can open his mouth. Voices start to call out, *When will you leave? How long before the others come back? Can we visit Ruthie?* They fall silent as the Shed door is flung open. The candles flicker wildly in the wind. Stace stands in the doorway, backlit by the moon.

"She's *my* best friend. If anyone is going to help Ruthie get to safety, it's me. I'm strong and I'm smart. And if you try to stop me then I will run after them and if you drag me back I'll try again and again and again." Stace is calm, her voice doesn't falter. She leaves, slamming the Shed door behind her.

PART TWO

Outside

I joined the Sanctuary before we gave it a name. In those days, it was just me and Zan and Eshe. To be saved by strangers after being forced out of your home by your loved ones has to be experienced to be believed. I get it; people are scared of dying and to some, the day we get the gift we stop being human. They find it easy to believe the wild stories about the Sanctuary, but we can't complain, that's what keeps us alive.

GREGOR, SANCTUARY

9

*Oral history? Are you joking? What do you want
to hear? That I was born with nothing, no one?
Left to die by parents who couldn't feed me? Not a
pretty story, is it, Logan? Your precious communities
never let me in. Roving was the only option for me,
I had no choice. I came to the City and the world
opened up for me. I was welcomed, for the first time
in my life. We have everything we need here. Houses
made of stone, plentiful food. I get it, the gift is a
blessing—for some—but what if everyone could do
it? You want to know what Saige is doing? Well,
there you have it. She's giving everyone a chance
to save themselves from starving. Put that in your
records. We're heroes.*

MAG, THE CITY

I come out of my room the next morning to find the
Recorder at our table. Logan wears the same old
coat, which, a long time ago, was the colour of May
blossom. Thick cotton, dusty with age and dirt, it's long
and loose on Logan's slim frame. Logan is either a man
or a woman; Mum says the work of recording our stories

95

for the generations to come is far more important than Logan's genitals.

"Take a walk with me, Ruthie." Hitching the familiar orange bag of papers onto a shoulder, Logan rises and holds out a hand. Logan's visits have been the best part of my childhood. When Joshie was taken, I turned to the Recorder to spill out my sadness, and watched as my words were scribbled on grey sheets of rough paper. Dad's ambush was harder to talk about. As the seasons flowed, my sadness dimmed but was never extinguished, and Logan was there to coax out my deeper feelings: anger at Mum and Owen, and finally, the burden of my gift.

As children, Stace and I played *who-wants-to-be-the-Recorder?* a lot; where we'd take turns to write down each other's tales of minor grievances. But Stace always preferred to talk, and I to write.

Mum gives me an apple and tries to smile.

In the Clearing we find Dad and Old Pete on the log bench, talking in low voices. They stand up when we enter.

"Talk in a bit?" Dad says to Logan, who takes his hand, smiles and nods.

"Of course."

On the bench Dad has just vacated, Logan takes a sheath of handmade papers covered with scratchy writing from the bag and hands them to me.

"I suspect you are more interested in my work than in telling your own story. You have the gift of listening, Ruthie."

Have I?

"Now that you're going on an adventure—"

"It's not an adventure," I say sullenly. The sky is grey this morning; I'm grey too. But the air is fresh and I take a deep breath. Squirrels run in between the tree stumps, pausing to beg for food. I can hear the smallies in the distance, playing catch-me-if-you-can, as if this is just another normal day.

"At your age I was wandering the length and breadth of the land with my mother," begins Logan and I sigh. This is going to be a story about how lucky I am. "I longed to stay in one place. And finally when I was of age to make my own decisions, I found I couldn't settle. When you are in a position to *choose* between one thing or another, that's when you begin to define *yourself*." Logan's smooth skin is suntanned. Bright blue eyes, a fine nose and full red lips make an interesting face, framed by short, spiky white hair.

"You have never had any great desire to leave the Field, and I hope the stories within these pages will give you comfort on your travels; they are the wise words of people who have lived hard lives. If you have the inclination to take a testimony or two of your own, there are blank pages." Logan finds a clean sheet and hands me a pencil. "Ready?"

I stare at Logan for a moment, confused, but then I lick the end of the stub of pencil as I have seen the Recorder do so many times, and nod. And Logan begins to speak.

"It is impossible to feel anything but joy on a day like today. The Field, in the late summer sunshine, sparkles."

* * *

On the night I left the Field, the moon hid behind dense grey cloud. Dad and I used wind-up torches to light our way across the Field. All the way to the Woods Dad had talked, in a low voice, about how he would never let anyone hurt me, that he was looking forward to this time together, to getting to know the woman I had become. And I felt the old love for him, I did. But at the same time, he was taking me away from the Field, from Mum and Ant.

People stood on their porches, calling out words of love and luck and then they went back inside to get on with their lives.

I blamed Mum for letting me go so easily. But maybe she hadn't, I thought, as we headed towards the dark Woods.

"In *two days*, Dan?" Back in the cabin after telling everyone in the Shed he was taking me to the Sanctuary, Dad was stony-faced while Mum cried. "Can't we take the week, at least?"

But Dad wouldn't meet her eyes. "We've made the decision. There's no point in drawing it out."

"*You* made the decision!" But Dad just looked out of the window into the Field. "I need more time," she said finally.

"I'm sorry, Gemma."

*   *   *

Seb and Dev and Stace were already at the edge of the Woods waiting for us, Owen walking away from them, towards home. When he sees me and Dad, he raises a hand to wave, touches it to his heart, but I ignore him.

As we enter the trees the pounding of footsteps at our backs turn us around. For the briefest moment, I imagine it is Mum, with Ant on her hip, a bag in her hand. But it is Mary, Stace's mum, instead. Wild hair, cheeks two dull red smudges.

When Stace had stormed out of the Shed that night, I watched her parents stare helplessly at each other. They knew as well as I did that she didn't plan to grow old in the Field. By the time Filip came by the next day to talk to Dad, I guessed they had decided it was better she left with friends than on her own. At least Dad had promised to bring her back.

Mary pulls Stace into her arms.

"Come back to us," she says. "Whatever you find, whatever you decide to do, promise to come back to us."

The Woods are a black silhouette against the night sky, growing smaller and smaller as Dad drives me away from the Field. One by one, Seb, Dev and Stace nod off. But I stay awake longer, looking back, trying to catch the last glimpse of my home before it vanishes.

"Ruthie?" Dad's voice is low, sad. "I know how this looks. That I came back just to snatch you away. But I hope you'll understand, maybe when you're older, that I had no option."

There is always an option, but Dad has decided that the choice was between either life with the Sanctuary or death. In time I hope those two *options* become as clear to me as they are to him.

*　　　*　　　*

The car is parked when I wake at dawn. Dad's low snores echo into the stuffy space. I don't open my eyes immediately, but try instead to imagine what I might see when I do. Will the world be a desolate grey blanket of brown grass, skeleton trees and the carcasses of long dead animals?

Instead of desolation, green light picks out a luscious landscape.

We are parked on one side of a long track of compressed leaves and brambles. Above us is a sky of green where the bushes and trees cross the track to hug. The colour grows more intense as light begins to flood the sky. Dev's skin takes on a yellow hue. The air smells of blackberries and rotting leaves and bright shrieks of birdsong fill the air.

"Amazing," Dev says.

Stace is already clicking open her door to step outside. One by one we leave the car.

"This is… This is…" she begins, then falls silent. Stace is breathing hard, her head turning slowly, to take it all in. It is as though we are moving through a dream as we pace the green track. We have leaves and birds in the Field, but this isn't the Field; the birdsong sounds more vibrant, the foliage greener, the leaves beneath our boots softer. I feel the tiniest prickle of excitement, for just a moment, overshadowing what lies ahead.

"Stace," I say, taking her arm. Her eyes are wide with wonder. "I'm glad you're here, you know." I gesture to the bridge of leaves overhead. "Imagine if you'd missed all this."

Stace laughs. "I'm not here for the trees, you idiot." She pulls me into her arms, only letting go when Dad calls us back to the car.

"We can stop again later," he says, grinning.

"Seen anything like this on a Supply Run?" Dev asks Seb when we are back inside the car.

"Nope," says Seb, shaking his head, his eyes still on the green canopy. "Just dry road and dead cars."

"Same."

The boys are laughing as Dad pulls away. Stace is staring out the back window, drinking in the last of the tunnel of green light as it gives way to open sky. The birdsong fades and once more the prospect of what lies ahead fills my mind.

"Ruthie?" Dad's voice seems to come to me from far away. "Owen teach you how to drive?"

I shake my head.

"OK then," he grins. "Once we're clear of Graylings *I* will."

"Graylings?" I ask. "What about the Coast?" Dad speeds up and my stomach clenches as he swerves the car between deep craters in the road.

This stretch of open road is lined with remnants of vehicles from before the Darkening—piles of scrap that aren't even good for salvage. Foliage has reclaimed these metal heaps and wildflowers spring from leather seats. Beyond are overgrown fields and beyond them hills covered with trees.

"I need to check in with someone," he says.

"This isn't the way to Graylings," says Dev, puzzled.

"There's more than one way to get there, Dev." Dad glances at his side mirror. I turn around, expecting to see another solar behind us, but the road is clear.

"Who are you meeting?" Dev asks. "Why?"

Dad sighs. "Ian," he turns his head to catch my eye, "a friend from the Circle." He rolls down his window and trails an arm in the hot wind.

Dev leans into the space between the two front seats. "Dan, come on. What's going on?" he asks.

Dad sighs again. "Nothing, Dev. Nothing is going on that has anything to do with the three of you." He says this like it's the end of the conversation, but Dev isn't done.

"Just leave it," I say, when he opens his mouth. "Dad knows what he's doing." Heat glimmers off the tarmac road and I'm too hot to think about the Circle. I'm too hot to think about anything.

"Does my dad know?" asks Seb, his eyes on the road ahead.

"Know what?" Dad doesn't look at him, but his jaw tightens.

"That we're going to meet the Circle, the vigilantes who—"

"Vigilantes?" Dev thumps Seb on the shoulder. "They're our only hope right now."

"Hope for what? A war we can't win?" Seb's voice is thin, high.

"You sound like Owen," I say, without thinking.

Seb whips round in his seat and I shrink back.

"And why is that so bad, Ruthie?" His face is red. "Is it because Owen is the monster who broke up your family?"

"Cut it out." Stace kicks the back of his seat.

"That's enough," snaps Dad. "I'm meeting Ian. He's Circle. And he's a friend who has helped me out in the past. That's all you need to know."

*   *   *

Three long hours later and the sun is a huge blister of heat in the sky. Our progress has been slow, the roads either a mess of potholes or a mess of woodland debris. Finally, we're climbing a steep track, green hills to our left and a low valley to our right. The path is more even. A blurry mountain range looms up in the distance, their tops hidden in the clouds. There are craters to navigate, but no rusting metal carcasses, they've all been tipped into the valley. There isn't a single other person or solar for miles. Dad is gripping the wheel like he hates it. We *all* feel exposed on this open road.

"This world is empty," he says, reading my thoughts.

A flash of light in the distance catches my eye. A tiny sliver of blue glistens at the edge of a small wood below the track. The sun is lower in the sky but still pumping out enough heat to melt us.

"We're going down," Dad says. "We could do with a break and the battery needs charging."

The car slows then stops.

Dad gets out and raises his binos. "A lake." We all strain to catch a glimpse. He pulls a hand-drawn map from his trouser pocket. "And another track we could take, if we go down." He shows us a faint grey line on the map leading out of the Woods, and then we're bumping down a hill of billowing long grass and dead cars. I'm trying not to think of the words *Sanctuary* and *Circle*. I'm trying very hard to pretend this is just a Supply Run.

The ground levels out and Dad parks at the edge of the woodland, an apple orchard; there is a sweet smell in the air. The forest floor is littered with over-ripe fruit.

"I'm taking a nap. Walk in the woods if you want," he says, pulling his sandy hat over his brow. "And no shouting."

I turn around as we enter the woods. The solar is charging, Dad is asleep. I'm about to splash cold water on my burning face. Stay in the moment, I tell myself.

Dev, Seb, Stace and I head into the trees. The sun shoots straight lines of blinding light through the leaves. In the distance an expanse of flat blue water glimmers through the branches; it looks perfect, like a child's drawing.

In seconds we're kneeling on stony ground, dunking our heads into icy blue. It's shocking and refreshing and for a moment I forget about being Giften, forget about the Sanctuary.

Icy water runs down my neck and back as I raise my face to the sun and shut my eyes. I stay that way for long minutes, hearing nothing, seeing only red beneath my eyelids. Dev flings a handful of cold water at me, and then another at Stace. She leaps on his back. They collapse onto the ground. Seb fills his leather pouch with water and pours it over them, I do the same. And then we're running through the orchard's cool shadows.

The noise of birdsong is loud; apples thud onto the ground around us, we slow down, crunching through rotten fruit and dry leaves.

"Stop." Dev holds up a clenched fist.

Above the birdsong, above the steady thump of apples, the rumble of a solar drifts into the woodland. Then doors slamming, hard voices. I start to move, panic rising. But Dev catches my arm. He crouches low, dragging me onto my knees. I try to struggle free, but he holds on tight. Stace is breathing fast. She falls to her knees beside me. Seb is still standing, trying to see through the trees.

"Get down!" hisses Dev.

I strain to make out snatches of words, but I can't hear anything above the pulse of my heart in my ears. I take slow breaths.

"Wait here." Dev stands up, letting go of me.

"No!" I say. "I'm coming too."

"Wait here, Ruthie!" Seb grabs my arm as I rise.

I shake him off and get to my feet. But Dev isn't moving. He raises a finger to his lips.

"He's alone," barks a voice, not Dad's. And the forest floor tips. I freeze. Every other thought exits my head. I need to get to Dad. But I can't seem to make my feet move.

"Sure about that?" says another. And then, "None of your Circle mates hiding out?" A snort of laughter.

MAGs!

"I was going home, that's all." Dad's voice. He doesn't sound scared. My heart leaps and the feeling comes back into my feet and I take a step.

"You're an escaped prisoner!" a voice shouts. I freeze again. My fingers start to burn. "You're not dumb enough to go home. Which is precisely why we've never looked for you *at home*."

"Fine," Dad says. "Let's go then. You don't need the ties. I'm not fighting you."

"Too right. Shall we light up the solar?" Another voice, gruff, mean.

"You crazy? Whole forest will go up. Let's just get out of here. I don't wanna wait around for his friends."

My hands are on fire. Dev crouches low and starts to move towards the voices. We follow, very slowly edging forward until we see four figures through the leaves; the MAGs in their black clothes look like giant crows against the lush green of the valley. Dad stands still as one MAG fixes a thin cord around his wrists, and yanks. My father is led out of sight. Car doors slam and the engine of a solar clicks to life. Then the rumble of a car driving through the long grass, and then silence. I watch all this in silence, powerless and immobile. I feel sick.

Through the trees I can see a grey solar sitting alone in the sunshine. It's impossible to believe he's not inside, his hat over his eyes, asleep. I snap out of it and suddenly I'm speeding towards Dad's car, praying for the impossible, but in seconds I'm on my knees, my feet caught in spiralling foliage. My hand lands on a single unripe apple, and I squeeze my fear into it and start to run again.

There is blood on the bonnet of the solar.

No one speaks for the longest time. I stare at the tracks in the grassy hill made by the MAGs' wheels, praying that Dad will appear over the lip of the road, waving as he makes his way back down to us.

"We need to turn this solar right around and go back to the Field," says Seb, finally. His lips are as white as his hair.

"Do you think they were following us?" Dev says, ignoring Seb. He meets my eyes. "We should go to Graylings," he says slowly. "Didn't Dan say this Ian guy was a friend? He'll want to know what's happened here. We should—"

"I agree," I say quickly. Of course that's what we should do. I need help. The Circle will help us. My head is spinning, but I have one very clear thought. "I'm not going back to the Field," I say. "I want to ask Ian for help." My nails dig into the apple, but the tingling in my fingers is only getting stronger. Anger is a red flame inside my chest. "I'm not losing Dad again."

"Ruthie!" Stace gasps, pointing at my hand.

The apple, once green and underripe, has turned into a handful of black charred flesh. I fling it away, my fingers are hot and pulsing, covered with rotting pulp. I shake it off, repulsed by the ashy mess.

"How…?" Stace whispers, staring at the apple's remains.

"I don't know," I whisper.

10

No more stories from me until we can walk freely all over this land. Until we can eat all the food we grow on our land. Until we have no fear that a solar driving into our communities is not full of men and guns. After that, I'll tell you where I'm from, who I was, and why I chose this path.

IAN, CIRCLE

e were stupid—the solar was in plain sight to anyone passing on the road, glinting in the sun, just like the lake.

Dev wipes a finger over a dull slick of dried blood on the bonnet.

"You should all go home," I announce, dully. "But I'm not giving up on Dad." I picture him in the Shed on the day of the storm, smiling, calling me *chicken*. It dawns on me that no one knows where we are. No one is coming to take me back to the Field or to the Sanctuary. I can go wherever I want.

"And what are *you* going to do?" Seb looks as sick as I feel. His skin is blotchy and pale. "Join the Circle? Rescue

Dan?" He doesn't want to be here; he doesn't want to be around any of this, I think.

"Yes, Seb," I tell him. "Both of those things." I turn to stare at the hillside once more. I picture Dad, tied up in the back of the MAG solar, wondering what we will do, thankful we stayed out of sight. He wanted to get out of here as fast as he could, before we showed up again. My heart thuds as his sacrifice becomes clear to me.

There's a moment's silence while the wind plays in the feathery grass, shifting it one way and then another. Cold sweat trickles down my back as I wait for one of them to speak.

"I'm in," Dev says finally. "So's Stace."

"No," I tell Stace. "This isn't what you signed up for." Now she's seen what an adventure looks like, she's bound to want to go home.

"*What I signed up for*? Are you serious?" She shakes her head. "I'm here for you. I'm *signed up*. Whatever you think about me, whatever you thought about me, you need to let it go." She's angry and I'm torn between wanting to shout at her and crying in her arms.

Dev is sweating, his eyes on fire as he turns to Seb.

"You?" he asks. And I think if I was Seb, if this had happened to Owen instead of my dad, I would want to go home. Back to the Field, sheltered by the Woods, surrounded by my family. He could forget about me, about Dad, build his cabin, find his One and Only. I don't care.

"OK, I'm in," Seb says, sighing. "Let's meet this Ian. For Ruthie. How good's your driving?" He's looking at Dev because Stace can't drive yet either.

"Better'n yours," Dev says.

*　　　*　　　*

Back inside the car, there are only four of us when there should be five. I slump into my seat while Dev rests the map on the wheel and stares at it in silence until Stace reaches between the seats and snatches it away from him.

"There's the track, remember?" She points to the grey line of road beyond the woodland and Dev starts the car. "I'll map read. Anyway, I thought you knew the way to Graylings."

"Not from *here*!" Dev sighs, checks his mirror and pulls away.

The grey line is a narrow track wide enough for a single solar. The bracken is bushy and tall on either side of us; purple flowers poke their heads above the green. Rabbits leap wildly in front of the tyres and skip away just as fast. The bracken gives way to woodland, a forest road of towering trees, shelter from the heat of the late afternoon sun.

We drive in silence as Dev navigates potholes and dead wildlife. My fingernails cut grooves into my palms until blood comes. Stace takes my hand.

"You need to calm down," Stace says, like it's easy.

"How?"

"We'll do this step by step, OK? You're not on your own."

Dev is staring at me from the driver's mirror.

"I don't know what we can do about saving him, maybe nothing. But Stace is right, step by step," he says.

My eyes well up, but no tears fall.

"What happened back there?" Seb asks. "With the apple?" He's trying to distract me, but I can't talk about the apple. This is what happens when you really upset the Giften, I think. They destroy the very things they are supposed to be nurturing.

"I don't know," I say. And then no one speaks for a long time.

There is so much *world* outside the Field, too much.

I'm exhausted, everyone is exhausted. This trip is over almost before it started. None of us should have left the Field. These thoughts roll around inside my head as the forest falls away and we're climbing another potholed tarmac road until it feels like we're on top of the world. Below us are wild fields of green and yellow grasses, clumps of woodland, wide lakes, and in the far distance a line of mountains, their snowy peaks touching the sky. In another valley we pass a dry lake bed in which the skeletons of a billion fish have crumbled into a fine white dust, as though new snow has just fallen, and a patch of land that must once have been a vast forest, but now is calcified ashes. I should be sharing these wonders with Dad.

My fingers tingle as the yearning to turn the burned land into green land overwhelms me. But how great is this gift, really? If Dad hadn't felt he had to take me away from the Field, he might still be here. I look away from the charred ground and sit on my hands. I wish the gift had happened to one of the others.

We drive past a great crack in the land into which buildings must have tumbled a long time ago, their stone chimneys and empty window frames jut above the gash.

"Quakes," Dev says. "Jacintha says the earth was so disgusted by everything we'd done to it, it just opened up and tried to swallow us."

*　　　*　　　*

As we draw closer to Graylings, Dev tells us we'll meet Salvage Sam whose house is a mile outside the community. He's a lonely sort, favouring his own company as he scouts for whatever scrap has survived the Darkening.

We haven't seen a single other soul on the roads. Dad was right, the world is empty.

On our approach we drive past a line of old stone buildings, and for the first time I see houses made of something other than wood. They look about ready to collapse, apart from one at the end, which is less of a ruin. There are piles of the old tech lying on the ground around the shelter: grey boxes, a mess of black cables, car parts and solar batteries.

"He isn't here," says Dev, stopping the car.

"He's Salvage Sam, so isn't he out looking for salvage?" Stace offers. She's holding my hand again, pressing her comfort into my bloody palm.

"Something's not right, though," Dev says slowly. "He usually leaves a sign to say whether he's home or away from home. There's neither. It's gone."

A cluster of curlews circle above us, their distinctive whistles breaking up some of the tension.

Dev starts the car, and we crawl slowly past the dilapidated buildings. Back on flat land, we follow a track through a field of tall yellow grass bathed in the light of the setting sun and then on to another track sloping downhill towards woodland. There is no wind, the trees are statues.

"Graylings," Dev announces. The car comes to a stop midway down a rocky path bordered by late summer lavender. The smell is strong and sickly, but I breathe it in, relishing its sweetness. Anything to distract the churning panic in my stomach. The sky is turning a cloudless pink on the horizon.

"You and I should take a look," Dev tells Seb.

"No!" I say, grabbing his arm. "We all go." I need to find Ian. He'll be here, in a cabin, waiting for Dad. And when I tell him what's happened, he'll want to help.

"We're not waiting for your permission, Dev," Stace says, clicking open her door.

"This isn't a gregious game, Stace," Dev fires at her. "Just wait."

"For the love of the land, will you calm down?" Stace has slipped out of the car and is striding ahead towards the woods.

Dev and I race to catch up but Seb is still in the car.

"I'll wait here," he calls. "Keep watch." Dev turns around, opens his mouth to object, but nods instead. He sprints ahead to lead the way.

Twigs snap under our boots as we step into the woods and out of the light. The curlews are back, flying in wide circles above the trees; their cries feel like warnings. Dev speeds ahead.

Where is Ian? Where is everyone?

"Dev, wait," I call.

"Something has happened here," he says, stopping, turning around. His voice is unsteady.

It's quiet and cool in the woods, the only noise is the rustling of birds in the leaves overhead. Dev's right. There is something very wrong here.

He starts to walk again, and we follow, until we're through the trees. We stand before a wide clearing around which stand seven wooden cabins. Washing lines cross the land, from one cabin to another, from which trousers, shirts and overalls hang, bone-dry, covered in bird shit. The chimneys are cold.

Dev takes the porch steps of the first house in the row in a single leap and disappears inside. I start to follow him, but Stace catches my wrist.

"Just wait, will you?"

He is back outside in less than a minute. One hand on the porch rail, he heaves and vomits.

And then Stace and I are running to him, each of us taking an arm as he stumbles down the steps.

"They're dead," he whispers. "Their heads... it's like they've exploded. We need to get out of here."

I stare around the deserted community. When did this happen? Are there dead bodies in each house? It's so peaceful that I don't feel afraid. Birds flutter in and out of the trees. Butterflies land on the clothes line and fly off. Two bumblebees chase each other across the clearing.

"But maybe someone's alive," I say. "Maybe they need our help."

"MAGs did this," Stace says, firmly. "What if they're still here?"

We hold still for a moment, listening. I can hear the sound of water running over stones. And then I'm moving towards the other cabins, racing up the porch steps, flinging open the doors.

They're empty.

Beyond the clearing, part of the forest has been cut away for cropland. The wheat, as yet uncut, sways in the wind, but the spinach has bolted and wide leaves of rhubarb lie flat and withered on dry soil. On the far side of the land a thin stream ebbs over pebbles as it winds its way into the woods. A wide squat shed sits at the edge of the woodland. As we draw closer we see the door is hanging off its hinges.

"Come on!" I say.

We cross the cropland and jump the stream, but as we approach the shed, a thick and sour smell and the sound of a million buzzing flies fills the air. And something else: lavender, blooming in stalky patches around the shed. Stace covers her nose with her shirt and I do the same. The light is fading fast, but Dev has his wind-up torch.

We pull open the heavy door and the single hinge holding it in place snaps. Dev catches the door before it falls, and the three of us lower it gently to the ground. The rough wooden surface has been punctured with bullets.

Dev shines his torch into the gloom. The ceiling is low, but it's a spacious enough storage room. In a corner the bodies of dead chickens lie in red splatters in their cages. I cover my nose with my hand, are they the reason for the smell?

But no. This is worse than anything I could have imagined, worse than anything Logan has ever recounted. Why did I want to see *this*? The bruised and bloody bodies of the Graylings community lie dead on the ground, side by side, men and women and smallies. Farm machinery is lined up against the far wall, bags of hard-won produce, potatoes, apples and flour, have been split open, their contents crawling with insects.

"Why?" My voice feels too loud in this room. No one should speak in here, ever. I taste bile at the back of my throat.

Stace buries her face in Dev's chest. But I don't turn away. I need to see this. I need to remember it.

"It looks like they fought back," I say, swallowing hard.

"It does," Dev croaks. He strokes Stace's hair.

"I want to see inside the first cabin." I head back outside.

Stace is looking at me as if I've lost my mind. The smell makes it hard to think. It surrounds me, it has soaked into my clothes, my skin, my hair. I draw in lungfuls of fresh air, only to inhale the stench of sweet lavender.

I know what I'm looking for; it's the most obvious of reasons: *they came for the Giften*. Is this why everyone is dead? Is this what would have happened to *us* if Daisy hadn't given up Joshie?

"I'm coming with you." Stace's trembling hand in mine. "We'll go in together."

We take the porch stairs slowly, gathering courage with each step. Inside the cabin, as Stace rears back from the blood and gore on the bed, on the walls and floor, I find what I'm looking for. A pot of soil on a nightstand. I stir my tingling fingers into the dry earth to reveal dead shoots. The earth gets wet fast. I raise a small handful of mud to my nose, as if it might tell me what happened here. But I know. There was a Giften here, and now, most likely *because of them*, there's no one here at all.

When we come out of the woods, the world stops moving. Seb is bent over the bonnet of Dad's grey solar, his face pressed into hot metal, the black-gloved hands of a MAG twisting his arms behind his back. Another MAG stands on the roof of our car, feet planted wide, sun glinting off the gun he's pointing at us; he's smiling.

11

I'd just caught some eels for our supper and I was coming up the sand track onto the road when I saw it. Near wet myself, I did. Two MAG solars on their sides, wheels spinning. I was frozen, couldn't even think to hide. The cars were full of MAGs. Covered in blood, they were, crawling out of their windows. And then these others leapt out of the grass on the other side of the road and swarmed them, killing every last MAG, either with an arrow or their fists. I watched the whole thing. When it was over, one of them turned to me and I thought, Here we go, Fred, it's you next. But she just smiles and says, "Tell your friends, the Sanctuary shows no mercy!" and hands me a bag of the most delicious veg I've ever tasted!

FRED, CROSSBILLS

 realize I've stopped breathing when my ribcage convulses, and I double over, hands on my knees, dragging in a breath.

"Steady now," the MAG with the gun says. "Weapons?"
The three of us stare at him blankly. Fear has frozen all

my senses. My head is empty. The MAG watches us and we watch him. None of us move for what feels like hours.

"Do. You. Have. Weapons?" he barks again. His words crack a sheet of ice in my skull. I have never spoken to a MAG, never had one look at me before, never been closer than twenty feet. And now, two of them are about to shoot us.

"We don't." Dev raises his hands, palms out. "We're… we're on a Supply Run."

"Come closer." The MAG on the roof beckons us with his gun and Dev and Stace start to move. I wonder where they're going, why they're leaving me. The ice is melting now, cold water sloshing around my head.

"All of you!" shouts the MAG, at *me*. He wants me to walk. Slowly, I put one foot in front of the other.

Seb watches us with one eye, his other pressed into the car bonnet, into Dad's dried blood. Parked behind the grey solar is the MAGs' shiny black car—passenger and driver's doors wide open. Heat radiates from the roof, the setting sun shimmers in the distance. MAGs have ambushed us. Is this so bad, I wonder. At least I'll see Dad soon. I shake my head to clear the crazy thoughts. My heart is thudding, my fingers itch and burn. Whatever trance I was in has vanished.

"Who are you?" The MAG tightens his grip on Seb, who flinches. He has a bald head, short red beard and heavy-lidded eyes, he looks like he's dozing.

"We're no one. Supply Run," says Dev. "Like I said."

"Community?" But Dev doesn't answer.

The other MAG jumps down from the roof of the car and hits the ground, raising dust. As one, we take a step back as he approaches. He has a tattoo of a spider on his neck, thin spindly legs reaching into his T-shirt. He taps Dev on the chest with his gun.

"Don't make me ask again." The MAG holsters his gun and punches Dev in the stomach.

Stace reaches out as if to block the MAG from hitting Dev again, but he draws back and slaps her hard across the face. Dev sinks to his knees and Stace stumbles into him, falling over. The MAG looks at me and the icy stream winds its way down my spine. The fear is a low hum which fills my whole body. I clench and unclench my fists to ease the tension in my fingers. The sky is red now, just like the MAG's face.

"We're from the Field," I croak. Something has happened to my voice.

"Good." The MAG turns his head. "You can let him go," he tells the other MAG. "Now, all of you, on your knees."

Dev is still trying to catch his breath, Stace's cheek is a blotchy purple. Released, Seb stumbles down the track.

"We won't give you any trouble," Dev wheezes, his hands in the dirt for support.

"So you're on a Supply Run, eh?" Red Beard asks. "Don't think there's much for you here unless you're collecting dead bodies." He gestures at the woods behind us with his gun.

"We didn't know," Dev says. "We'll go back home now."

"You Circle?" the tattooed MAG asks.

"We're nothing," Seb says. "We don't have any weapons. We're just four kids."

Four kids. He's right and he's wrong. At that moment, my fear becomes something else, something hotter than the sun, colder than the water in the lake.

"What do you want?" I say steadily. "We said we're on a Run, and you're right, there's nothing here for us and now we want to go home."

"On your feet!" Spider Neck yells.

I stand slowly. His gun is still in its holster, but he doesn't need that to kill me, he could do it with a single punch. I raise my eyes to his. I'm looking at a MAG and a MAG is looking at me.

"Your solar." He points over his shoulder. "A little while ago colleagues of ours captured an escaped prisoner driving that same car. And now it's here." He takes a step towards me but I don't move as he leans in. His breath smells like stale vomit.

"He was from the Field. You're all from the Field. You're about the same colour as him, you his kid?"

And then the fear is back. My bravery crumbles.

"Your dad is a spy and a traitor. He's been running from us for a year, but look around you," he indicates the wide empty fields, the woodlands, the sky, "there's nowhere to hide where we can't find you." He laughs as the sweat pours down his forehead. "I'm going to take you back with me and when your dad sees how you squeak when I squeeze you, he'll tell us where all the other spies and traitors are." There's spittle at the corners of his mouth. He is triumphant.

Time slows down as he raises his hand high in the air. It begins its arc towards my face, and then… stops.

His mouth is wide open but no sound comes out. From the lavender bushes, an arrow has flown through the air into the side of his neck, straight through his spider tattoo. As if it were a target.

We stagger away from each other. The MAG wraps his fingers around the tip and the shaft; blood spurts from two holes. I can't look away. I'm aware of Dev moving past me, leaping at Red Beard, who is turning around to aim his gun into the bushes. But Dev is on his back, knocking him off his feet. They crash to the ground. The Spider is writhing around in the dust, gurgling and spluttering, his face a crazy mask of pain.

Dev straddles Red Beard's chest, his hands around his neck. Stace springs up from her knees and kicks the MAG hard in the ribs, over and over. And then I'm moving too, stamping on his wrist until he releases the gun. I grab it and launch it into the bushes.

The tattooed MAG is dead, his face and hands and neck are coated in congealing blood. It flows into the dirt, making mud. His gun still in its holster.

Red Beard thrashes and curses and chokes as Dev's grip tightens.

"Hold up there!" a voice calls.

Stace and I whip around. The voice came from the bushes. I wish I had held on to the gun. Seb is still on his knees staring at the dead MAG as three figures emerge from the dense thicket of lavender. A boy with spiky blond hair is rubbing his head and holding up the gun I had just thrown into the bushes.

"That really hurt," he says, grinning.

12

Five years ago it was, and we still light a candle, say a few words to remember the dead. We were the first to hear what happened on Ravelston Road, living near the City as we do. Word came down that the MAGs had been travelling in convoy to the Base when the Circle attacked—rigging up some explosives—killed everyone on board. What they didn't know is that there was captive Sanctuary on those trucks too. But Circle did what they do and left everyone for dead.

TANAYA, HILLWOODS

Two boys and a girl, around Dev and Seb's age, stand on the track, wild lavender at their backs. None of them seem bothered by Dev grappling with a MAG in the dust. One of the boys has a bow in his hand, a small holster for arrows on his hip.

I move slowly, I have only a moment to do this if I'm going to do it. I whip away from the strangers and lunge for the dead MAG's gun, ripping it from his belt. I scramble to my feet, aiming a weapon I have no idea how to use. But we haven't just escaped capture by MAGs to be ambushed by... by...

"Hey," says the boy with the spiky hair. I point the gun at him. "We're not the enemy, OK?" He nods to the other boy, the one with the arrows. "Young Noah here just saved your lives." My aim doesn't waver.

Noah bows.

"You're welcome." He grins and points at the weapon and I swing it round to aim at him instead. "Would you mind?" he asks.

"Ruthie!" Stace pushes the gun aside slowly.

I stare at the three strangers. Not the enemy?

Noah is looking at the dead MAG and the half-strangled MAG beneath Dev, who is coughing and clutching his neck. "Is this all of them?" he asks, his eyes sweeping the scene.

"Just these two," says Seb.

"You can get off him, you know. He can't hurt you now," Noah tells Dev.

Dev raises a fist and brings it down hard into the side of the MAG's head, punching him unconscious. For a moment I marvel at the violence in Dev's hands. Hasn't he always just lived in the Field, like me? When did he get so tough?

"You're all from Graylings," I say, wondering who is going to tell them their community has been slaughtered.

The blond boy shakes his head. "No. We're supposed to be meeting a friend," he waves a hand to the woods at the foot of the hill, "instead we find… Well, I'm guessing you know what happened back there." He sighs, wiping a hand over his face, over his spiky hair. "So we decided to drive around rather than wait here, in case whoever did this came back." He points at Dad's car. "You're driving his solar," he says.

"You're Ian?" I say. "From the Circle?"

He smiles and gestures towards the girl.

"And this is Mairie." Mairie is my height and has the same chestnut skin. Her dark hair is cropped short. She wears a belt made of foxtails. "And you've already had the pleasure of Noah."

"You were meeting my dad." Now that Ian's here, everything else falls away for the briefest moment; the dead MAGs, even Graylings.

"Might be," he says. "Where is he anyway?"

A lump fills my throat and I can't answer.

Stace winds her arm around my shoulders. "MAGs," she says. "They ambushed him."

Ian sighs and Mairie shakes her head.

"Damn," he says. "That is not good. We needed him in one piece."

Mairie shoots him a warning look. "Hey, don't start shooting your mouth off," she says, taking his arm. "You always talk too much."

"She's Dan's kid," says Ian. "She's no threat to us, Mairie."

"But he's not." Mairie points at Noah.

"Noah's not our enemy. He wants the same thing," snaps Ian. "He's just not prepared to help us fight for it."

I hand Dev the gun which he shoves into the waistband of his trousers.

"I'm not with them. I'm not Circle," says Noah, to me. He fixes his bow to his back. His hair is so short, it's just a dark patch all over his head. His face is covered in stubble; a single dimple appears in his cheek when he smiles, and something catches in my chest. His clothes are made from the remnants of other clothes like ours, but consist of only three colours. Green, deep yellow and grey.

"Met him on the road," Ian says. "He hitched a lift as we were all going the same way."

"*You're* from Graylings?" I ask Noah, but he shakes his head.

"I'm Sanctuary. Meant to be picking up a Giften boy from here. Ian told me what happened, but I needed to come and see it for myself, so here I am."

I'm not interested in his story; he can't help me. But I was right, all this happened because of a Giften child.

"It's not what—"

I hold up a hand and he stops talking. "Can you help me find my dad... find Dan?" I ask Ian.

"Ruthie, wait!" Seb's voice is sharp. "Please. We should go home. Tell Owen, *he* will help us, he—" Seb's white hair hangs in damp strands around his face. He's pale and sweaty. I wish he wasn't here.

"Seb, for the love of the land, what do you think Owen is going to do?" Stace says, her voice is shaky like she's about to start crying. "How is Owen going to put this right? Go. And. Look. Owen can't fight the MAGs alone. No one can."

Seb holds her gaze for a long moment and then turns on his heel, heading for the woods.

"Hold up," calls Noah, following him down the track.

"Help me load their bodies into the solar," Ian tells Mairie. "Then we'll light it up by the cabins."

"Wait. Didn't you hear me?" I say. "I want to find my dad."

"Later," says Ian. They haul the tattooed MAG into the back of the black solar.

Afterwards, they check inside the car, retrieving food, more guns, boxes of ammunition. They dump the stuff into their backpacks hidden in the lavender bushes and then move towards Red Beard, who's still unconscious; gasping snores stream from his wide open mouth.

"Wanna do it?" Ian asks Mairie, who nods, pulling out a gun from her belt. Stace and I jump back as the gun explodes, scattering birds into the sky. Blood soaks the front of Red Beard's black shirt.

In silence, Stace, Dev and I watch them load him into the front seat of the solar. Mairie climbs into the car and drives it into the woods, passing Noah and Seb heading back up the track.

There isn't a cloud in the sky. We're bathed in the fading red light of the setting sun. The smell of lavender wafts through the air and I think about dead bodies. My stomach turns.

"Maybe the kid got away," says Noah, rubbing a hand over his shorn head. He means the Giften boy he came to rescue.

"Maybe he's dead in the shed with everyone else," I say. What's the point of optimism in this place? But isn't that just what I'm doing? Hoping Ian and the Circle will rescue Dad.

"I guess I'll be on my way then." The dimple is gone.

"Back to your hidey hole?" says Ian. "Back to safety and security?"

Dev is staring at me, but the Sanctuary was Dad's dream, not mine.

"What is it, Dev?" I snap. "You still want to dump me with the Sanctuary? After all this?"

"No!" says Dev. "Of course not. But Dan wanted you safe. We should talk about it at least."

"I need to find Dad. Right now, I don't care about being Giften." I gesture at Noah. "And I don't care about the Sanctuary."

"You're Giften?" Noah's eyes are grey. No one in the Field has grey eyes.

I nod.

"You could work with us, Noah," Ian says, pulling the bloody arrow he had yanked out of the MAG's neck from his belt. Noah takes it and slides it into the holster with all the others. "What happened on Ravelston Road, that was a long time ago. We're not those people. MAG numbers aren't that high by our reckoning, not more than five or six hundred. The Circle is three hundred strong now and your lot could make all the difference to our fight. It's time to organize. You've seen Graylings, you know things are getting worse." Ian squeezes Noah's arm. "Change your minds."

They are planning a war. I stumble in the dust. What have we walked into?

I know about Ravelston Road. A story from a lifetime ago. A convoy of MAG trucks ambushed by the Circle who killed everyone, including fifty members of the Sanctuary who had just been ambushed themselves. I was only ten when the news reached the Field. But it was enough to set some of the communities against the Circle.

"I'd do it, Ian. I'd help you," says Noah. "But I can't speak for the couple hundred other Giften in the Sanctuary."

"Work with you how? Organize what?" Dev says, looking from one boy to the other.

"They're going to attack the Base. The MAG house," says Noah, not taking his eyes off Ian. So, this was Dad's plan all along. To leave me with the Sanctuary and return to the City to start a war.

Seb is groaning. His face is green, and then he is on his knees, vomiting onto the track, his body heaving.

"You *should* join them," I tell Noah. "You can fight. *Everyone* is scared of the Sanctuary. What, for the love of the land, could be more important than getting rid of the MAGs for ever?"

"There's history," he says. He nods at Ian. "He knows."

"Precisely, Noah! History!" Ian throws up his arms. "We've changed. Take her back with you. Let her tell them what she's seen here. She's Dan's kid, he's solid Circle, but he's also a friend to your people. How many Giften's he saved now?" *Wait.* Take me back?

"No idea," says Noah. "And I've never met him. The twins know him though. Say he's solid, for a Circle."

"That's settled then." Ian claps his hands.

"No!" I say. It's like I'm not even here. "Nothing's settled. I'm not going to the Sanctuary. That's over. I'm coming with *you*," I tell Ian.

"But Ruthie—" Stace begins.

"But nothing, Stace. My dad is in the City, and I don't know where *he's* going," I nod towards Noah, "and I don't care."

Ian and Mairie are shaking their heads. "If you want to help us, if you want to get your dad back, stick with Noah," Ian says. "Dan is the only link we have with the Sanctuary. It makes sense. Look at the signs, Ruthie. He's *your* dad, not Noah's." Ian turns to Dev. "But this guy should come with us. If you want to." He glances at Seb, who's wiping his mouth, and at Stace. "The Field isn't too far from here, I guess we could take the other two back. Noah and Ruthie can take Dan's car."

"Guess again," Stace says, hands firmly on her hips.

"I'm sticking with Ruthie." She looks at Seb, at Dev and then at me. "Have you all forgotten who else might be in the City?"

Dev stares back at her with wide eyes. He clears his throat.

"None of us have forgotten Joshie, Stace," he says. "But one thing at a time. OK?"

Noah runs a hand over his scalp and stares into the setting sun. An explosion in the woods spins us around. Smoke rises above the trees. The MAG solar is on fire. Mairie is running up the track.

"I'll take her," says Noah, grinning at me. "Maybe she *could* make a case—"

"And we're staying together," Stace says. She looks at Seb.

"I'm sticking with Ruthie too," he says quietly. I can hear the hesitation in his voice. He's not brave like Dev, or angry like Stace, or cornered like me. He could go back and no one would blame him.

I wait for the anger, but it doesn't come. I think about my options. What do I have to lose by talking to the Sanctuary, telling them about Graylings, about the lives lost because of one Giften boy? I wonder what Dad would advise if he was here. I make up my mind. If it doesn't work, at least I will have tried.

"Ruthie…" Dev begins.

"It's OK, Dev," I say. "Go with Ian. One way or another I'll see you in the City."

He takes me into his arms and whispers in my ear. "You're a fighter, Ruthie. So fight for this and you'll never be sent away again."

"I wish I was coming with you," I whisper back. And I do. But if there is even a small chance that I could get Dad back *and* help to defeat the MAGs, then I'd be a fool not to try.

"You have a week," Ian says, pulling a crumpled scrap of paper from his pocket. Mairie hands him a pencil, shaking her head. "Timing is everything. Soon the MAGs will leave the Base in hordes to collect the harvest Offerings. It has to be now, while they're all still in one place." He leans against the bonnet of the grey solar and starts to write.

"This is where we'll be in the City. Come and find us when you're ready," he says, handing the scrawled note to Noah. He catches his hand as he takes the paper. They lock eyes. "You have to forget the past. Tell them... tell them we're sorry."

Even though we're four in the car again, two of us are missing now. Who's next, I wonder. Noah is at the wheel because he knows where he's going. But I don't. In the space of a couple of hours, we've joined the Circle and promised to bring the Sanctuary to the City. Somehow we have to get two hostile factions to resolve their wounded history. And then, together, they will have to fight an army of MAGs. Somewhere in that mess is my dad, waiting to be saved.

We have a week, that's all.

I watch Ian, Mairie and Dev emerge from the lavender bushes in a black solar. Perfect camouflage. Dev, in the back, locks eyes with me and spreads his palm across the window; I do the same. And then they're gone.

Last night I slept in my own bed in my cabin in the Field. Now, as Noah bumps along the stony path out of Graylings, driving into the cloud of dust thrown up by Ian's wheels, I'm not thinking about where I'll sleep tonight, but if I'll ever sleep again. I catch Noah's eye in the driver's mirror.

"Ever been on an island?" he asks, smiling.

13

*I woke to find myself in the City. I was fifteen, and
had never been outside my lakeside community until
that day. But I wasn't afraid. Not of the MAG who
had half strangled me as he forced me into the solar;
or of the City, and its cadaverous buildings. With a
clarity that comes only once or twice in a lifetime,
I knew that if he got me into the Base I was never
coming out. The ivory hilt of a knife, tucked into
his waistband, caught the sun. It called to me. I felt
nothing as I stuck him. He was my first MAG.*

XANDRIA, OTTOWAY

The wheels of Dad's car turn, taking us ever closer
to the coast. He told me he came back because,
The desire to see you, Ruthie, was too strong. But
really, he had come back to say goodbye, in case he died
in the attack against the Base. Something hard and small
and bitter twists inside me; if he was going to die anyway,
whether at the hands of the MAGs who ambushed him,
or in battle with MAGs in the City, I wish, for the briefest
of moments, he hadn't come back at all. Mum thought

he was dead, and in time I would have come to believe the same. Right now, I don't know if I'm angry or sad. But a new hope springs inside my chest too, one I hadn't allowed myself to think about until Dev said his name at Graylings. Maybe Joshie is in the City too. Waiting to be rescued.

Stace, up front with Noah, pores over Dad's map, retracing our journey with her finger. We pass the same landmarks, but everything is different. I am exhausted but sleep is the last thing on my mind. If I even blink, the images of the dead appear, as if burned onto my retina. And the tracks in the grass from a black solar taking my dad to the City.

"We should sleep," Noah announces. "In about an hour we'll come to Farm Down. It should be safe."

We are in a valley, trees stand tall along the ridge of the hills, throwing long shadows off into the foothills, moonlight bounces off abandoned farm machinery, junked cars.

The road climbs out of the valley into a woodland of larch. Their needles are black spikes.

There is a very rough track through the woodland, Noah plunders on through purple thistle, the solar bumping stones as he forges ahead. Quick movements in the undergrowth reveal skittering rabbits. I eye Noah's bow in the footwell.

"Can you catch a rabbit for dinner?" I ask. I want to talk about normal things, for a moment at least. The weight of my mission is too heavy right now to think about.

He smiles in the gloom. "Maybe."

We park the solar in the trees and the four of us start to walk. The night is warm and in minutes my pack is stuck to my back. It doesn't feel like there's another person in the world. The air is alive with insects and alien birdsong. My hands pulse to the tune of my heartbeat. I drop behind the others to grab a handful of forest debris; the soil and leaves and tiny twigs sift through my fingers and my pulse slows. But Noah slows down too, and bends to do the same. His grey eyes are black in the dim light.

"How long?" he asks.

"A year."

"They couldn't hide you?" The earth becomes wet in his hands. I shake my head slowly.

"Not really. You?"

"A story for another time." He grins. "You're pretty brave, you know."

I swallow hard, and pull my hands from the earth. "Not really," I say.

"Really," he says, flinging mud off his fingers, wiping them on dry leaves. "I'd like to hear your story too, maybe."

"Where are we going?" Seb calls in the distance. "You're meant to be leading us, Noah!"

Noah dumps the earth. "He's fun," he says, taking my arm. I startle at his touch, but he's only steering me around a rabbit hole. "There'll be dirt at the farm too," he says.

There's a different silence in these woods, leaves swish and stir in the faint breeze, it's cooler now and I find myself wishing we could just lay our mats here on the ground, but it's alive with biting bugs.

I keep my attention focused on what's in front of me, otherwise I find myself drifting back to the broken bodies of brave people, smelling their despair or imagining Dad in a dungeon, dying of thirst. One step at a time.

The trees fall away and we're walking through long grass towards a collection of crumbling stone buildings. Black shapes in the dusk. They are dotted about a scrub of what was once fertile farmland, now it's just weeds, thistle and patches of scorched earth. I try to imagine horses running through the field beyond, but I can't.

Noah leads us into a building with most of its roof intact, a single hole in the centre of the ceiling lets in a single thin shaft of moonlight.

"Light a fire outside," says Noah, taking the bow from his back.

"I'll collect some wood." Stace follows him out of the room.

I start to lay out mats on the ground. From our packs I remove dried fruit, apples, a loaf of bread and water, while Seb watches me.

"Ruthie, how can you be OK with this?" he asks, break-ing the silence. He swipes at cobwebs in the corners of the room with his sweater. "I'm supposed to be keeping you safe, but you won't let me."

I need to be outside, my hands in the dirt again. "OK with what, Seb?" I round on him. "OK with trying to get Dad back? Is that what you mean?"

He looks at me with helpless eyes. I picture him in the kitchen at home, happy making supper, happy whittling arrowheads.

"Come on," he says. His face is flushed and he waves a hand around the room. "You know that's not what I mean. You know—"

"Seb, please," I say. "I don't know. I don't know if this is a huge mistake or the only way forward." I drop the apple I'm holding, suddenly terrified I might shrivel it. "We just need to eat and sleep. OK?"

He opens his mouth but shuts it again when Stace pokes her head into the room.

"I've got the wood," she says, her eyes moving between me and Seb. "All good?"

I nod and follow her outside.

She places small twigs on the ground and covers them with dried leaves. I set out the food while she uses her flint and steel kit on the fire, until the leaves spark and catch. Seb is a shadowy figure in the doorway.

"What's going on with you?" Stace asks him.

"Nothing," he mumbles. "I'm just hungry."

She throws him an apple and he grins a *thank you*, biting into its flesh.

"And I have food!" Noah announces, stepping into the light of the fire. He holds up two dead rabbits.

*   *   *

Not even the soft snores of Seb and Stace can coax my eyes shut. Something skitters across the floor, there's a soft rustling outside. The moon hovers above the hole in the ceiling; there's enough light to make out the figure beside me; Noah is awake too. He sits up slowly and holding a finger to his lips he reaches for his bow.

"Wake the others," he mouths.

The rustling outside is louder. The crunch of dry leaves, twigs snapping.

Stace and Seb rouse at my touch. Stace reaches for her gun and for a moment I wonder where she got it, and then I remember. Ian offered me a gun too, but I wouldn't take it. We follow Noah, on tiptoe, out of the room. My heart is thudding so loud I think the others can surely hear it. But it's a different fear to yesterday, at Graylings. MAGs would have just blundered in, firing guns.

"Probably just a deer," whispers Seb.

But there's no one outside, no MAG solars hidden in the trees, no black-clad figures jump out of the bushes, no deer. The crunching has stopped. The moon passes behind a cloud. Trees creak in the wind; bright green horse chestnuts drop at our feet.

"Stay here," Noah says. He points at Stace's gun. "Be ready."

Stace nods, her mouth a thin line of determination.

"Ready for what?" whispers Seb, but Noah is creeping away, rounding the side of the building; his footsteps are slow and steady to begin with and then they pick up pace; the rustling grows louder. Someone is running. I suddenly feel very cold. Maybe Noah isn't moving at all and someone else is out there, running towards *us*. I imagine Noah dead. Stace, Seb and I captured.

Stace starts to move, but Seb catches her arm.

"Wait," he says.

But she jerks free, the gun held out before her.

"Hold up!"

We freeze at the sound of Noah's voice; too loud in the silence. Slowly we edge around the building.

"We don't want to hurt you," Noah is saying. "Just come out." He's standing in front of a tangle of blackberry bushes, his bow hanging limply from his hand.

"Noah," I hiss, "what are you doing?" The panic comes now. My mouth is dry. I gulp in air. Stace aims her gun at the bushes, with a trembling hand. Noah pushes it aside.

"It's just a kid. He threw himself in the brambles." He moves towards the bushes, parting the thorny branches, reaching inside until he comes away holding the hand of a child.

The clouds shift and moonlight reveals a young boy, his arms covered in long bloody scratches. His face is filthy, tears smudged in dirt, torn clothes. But it's his fear that draws me towards him. He can't be more than six years old. My heart is no longer hammering; instead it aches for this boy.

"Are you alone?" I ask, kneeling in front of him. He nods and his face crumbles as he throws his arms around my neck and begins to sob. My hands fold around his thin body and I pull him close.

"I ran… I ran away," he says, his chest heaving. "Mum made me. The MAGs…" And then I know who he is. He's the missing Giften child.

"You ran all the way from Graylings?" I whisper into his ear as Noah, then Stace kneel on the ground beside me.

"They caught me and put me in their solar, but when they stopped to… to pee, I ran away into the woods. They couldn't find me because I squeezed into a fox hole."

"You did really well, kid," Stace says, stroking his hair. "You're safe now." The boy's arms are tight across my back, as though he will never let go. "What's your name?" she asks.

"S-Scottie," he's hiccupping now and I ease him away.

"Are you hungry, Scottie?" Noah asks. He lays his bow on the ground and takes the boy's hand, rising from his knees.

Scottie raises big tearful eyes to Noah, and nods. "And then can you take me home?"

"I went to Graylings to find *you*, Scottie. I'm taking you to a new home, where you'll be safe. This is Ruthie, she's coming too."

* * *

After we'd fed Scottie, after Stace had told him the MAGs had overrun Graylings, that his parents were probably dead and his community was gone, I rocked his shuddering body to sleep but I still lay awake. The smallies grow up knowing loss; losing parents, loved ones to illness or starvation. Brutal truths hurt just the same, but great tragedy isn't ever a surprise.

I wake before dawn and, pulling Logan's oral histories from my bag, I slip outside to read by the light of the moon. I lose myself in the stories of famine and plenty, of grief and loss and joy and love, until my eyes finally start to close again.

"What are you reading?" Noah crouches beside me. My eyes snap open. I show him a sheet of paper.

"Logan's work," he says, taking the page. He sits down next to me, our backs against a dusty wall that was built long before our great grandparents had been born. "This one's a poem," he says.

"Scottie is young for a Giften, isn't he?" I ask.

Noah looks up from the page. "He is, but it's not uncommon." He turns back to the poem. "It's a strange one, this." Noah sighs and hands me back the sheet of paper. "The gift is different for everyone, when it happens, how it changes for some."

"Changes? How?" Are there other Giften who can shrivel food with their touch, instead of growing it?

"Wait till we get to the Sanctuary," he says. "You'll meet Zan, our leader. She can show you."

I drift off while Noah reads by moonlight and dream about Fred from Crossbills who witnessed a convoy of MAGs attacked by a group of nomads, who speared the necks and cracked the skulls of two carfuls of MAGs. I dream about Xandria from Ottoway, a fifteen-year-old girl, just like me. She plunged the MAG's own knife into his body and escaped, drenched in his blood.

It's past dawn when Noah gently nudges me to wake up. I had fallen asleep on his shoulder. I jerk away.

"We need to get moving. The MAGs will come back for the kid."

And like that, any safety I felt, blinks out.

14

The dawn watch raised the alarm; a boat was steaming towards the Island. It had to be MAGs, they couldn't even sail in a straight line. But we let them come into the bay, let them slip and slide their way onto solid ground, big guns on their shoulders. We let them feel like they had a fighting chance. They hadn't even made it halfway up the hill when we attacked. Then we sent a boatload of dead MAGs back to the mainland. They never returned.

ESHE, SANCTUARY

Scottie dozes in the car and then he wakes up, bleary-eyed and disorientated. I see the panic in his eyes as he tries to work out why he's in a solar full of strangers. But when he looks at me, something eases in his face. He leans into me, and I wrap an arm around his shoulders, drawing him closer.

"Will I be safe in the Sanctuary?" he whispers, but the truth is, I don't know.

"Course you will, kid," says Noah, turning his head to wink at the little boy in the back.

The road spins on through a tunnel of impossibly long yellow grass.

I listen to Stace telling Noah about the Field, about her dad who makes furniture and toys, bows and arrows. She tells him about Tobes, her little brother, and about Old Pete and Lucia. She asks him about the island.

"It's just one of our bases," he's saying. "Our leader is there right now."

"But where do you live?" Stace persists.

"Here and there." Noah grins, catching my eye. "You'd love our base in the City. The Tombs. Stinky, dark, underground rooms. Very atmospheric." He yawns.

"Want me to take over?" asks Seb.

Noah slows the car and brakes. "I think the girls should drive. Want me to teach you?" he says, shifting round in his seat, a wide smile on his face.

So, instead of Dad, it is Noah who positions my hands on the wheel and directs my feet to the right pedals. When at last I pull away, Stace and Seb watch us from the side of the road.

Stace waves and yells, "You're driving, Ruthie!"

My heart fills for a moment. It feels great. This taste of freedom was all Stace wanted; something new in her predictable life.

But, of course, Stace is already a brilliant driver. When it's her turn, she takes off before Noah can open his mouth, shooting up the dusty track, expertly turning the car around and screaming back up the road.

"Filip taught you, didn't he?" I ask when she steps out of the car.

Noah's head is in his hands.

"Maybe," she laughs. "Just a bit."

"Just *a lot*," says Seb. He ruffles Scottie's hair. "Can you drive too?"

But Scottie shakes his head.

"You never told me," I say, peeved.

Stace looks surprised. "Dad said not to tell, but, I don't know, I didn't think you'd be interested."

"Really?" I know I'm being silly. I know I have more to worry about than Stace's secrets, but right now, it hurts. "Why?" She doesn't meet my eyes.

Noah hovers behind her, staring into distant woodland.

Seb's eyes are on his boots. "Because she thought you'd tell her off," he says.

"*You* knew?" I'm shocked. I feel a lump in my throat.

"Don't say that, Seb!" Stace snaps. "That's not the reason."

"What then?"

"Because you don't like breaking the rules, that's why," she says sullenly. "I'm sorry. OK?"

"Come on," says Noah, wearily. "We need to get going. You can sort this out in the car."

*   *   *

It's late afternoon; the sun is low in the sky and pink streaks paint the horizon. I taste blood on my lips, having sunk my teeth into them every time I have to steer the solar around a gaping crater. Stace is in the passenger seat, staring glumly out of the window. I reach over and pat her hand, my eyes on the road.

"Stace. We're good, right?" I say, and she nods, but doesn't look at me.

"I'm an idiot," she whispers. "I didn't mean that stuff… about the rules. I just wanted one secret, my own thing. I didn't even tell Seb, you know. He saw us one day, me and Dad, driving through the Woods. That's all."

My own thing. I should be able to understand that. I have *my own thing* too; something I kept secret from most of the community. But I'm not like Stace, I didn't like my secret one bit.

"I get it," I lie. "I do."

*　　　*　　　*

On a wide road, flat land to the left and right of us, we pass a junk heap of old cars, metallic monsters, overgrown with vegetation, homes to wildlife, adorned with the late wildflowers of autumn.

"We'll be on the coast by sunset," Noah says.

"And then what?" asks Seb.

"Then I'll send up a signal and someone will come and meet us."

"Who?" Seb's voice is calm; you'd have to know him to tell that he's edgy, scared.

I hear Noah sigh.

"Someone from the Sanctuary. I don't know who exactly."

The landscape changes again. A crumbling stone wall follows the road, beyond which are scrubby bushes and forlorn trees that look like they're dying.

Above us starlings form patterns in the sky as they dive one way and then another. Huge rocks begin to dot the landscape, imposing and grey.

"We're nearly out of power." Stace taps the dashboard. "How much further?"

Noah leans between the two front seats and points up the hill we're slowly climbing.

"If we can make it to the top, I'll send the signal."

High in the hills, we park in the centre of a cluster of boulders nestled in lush green grass. Tall trees beyond the rocks are bent double from years of resisting the wind. And there is the sea; an expanse of water larger than my imagination. Through the windscreen I stare and stare and stare at it. One of my old books, its pages swollen by time and moisture, had faded drawings of the sea, grey and dull and vast. My eyes drink in a scene that has nothing in common with those dusty pictures. An orange haze sits on the horizon, throwing a yellow glow over the water. Close to shore, foaming waves buckle and overlap as they race towards the land. Did Dad see the sea on his way home? I hope so, I hope he has this memory wherever he is, because it is magnificent.

We sit in silence for long minutes watching the sea, until Scottie clambers into the front seat and onto Stace's lap.

"Can we go in?" he asks. He sounds like a normal little boy, excited by this new miracle.

"Too cold," says Noah. "Maybe tomorrow. From the Island." The word *island* breaks the spell and one by one we get out of the car.

The grass is short and springy beneath my feet. The ever-present tingling in my fingers eases for a second as I dig down to find the soil. Scottie joins me, his small hands ploughing furiously.

"This will warm you up," I tell him.

The sun is setting over the water; the sky is now a cold, milky yellow.

"It might be too dark for them to see the smoke," Noah announces, gathering small branches to light a fire. "We may have to sleep here tonight, wait for the battery to charge tomorrow and drive down to the beach in the morning where I can light another fire."

"Ruthie, up here," calls Stace. She has climbed the largest boulder. "I can see everything! I can see the Island."

"Seb!" I call, climbing up. And then the three of us are staring at a hump of green in the sea.

"It's beautiful," Seb says. "It looks like the Field."

We watch Noah head off with Scottie further up the hill, into a cluster of rocks, a bow slung around

Scottie's thin back. Before they disappear, the boy turns around.

"Ruthie, you come too, Noah is going to show me how to shoot arrows."

"I'm going to get some food together," I say. "Anyway, it's too dark to be shooting arrows."

*   *   *

Later, taking out canopy poles from the boot of the solar, I call for Stace and Seb to make the shelter.

"Where's Seb?" Stace asks, taking the poles from me.

"No idea," I say. "We should eat. I'll fetch the others." I head for the rocky outcrop. My hands are still tingling, five minutes in the earth wasn't enough. I need hours and hours. As I round a large boulder expecting to find Scottie and Noah, I see something else instead. Something that makes no sense.

There are two girls, two *identical* girls, older than me, taller than me. Their hands are held high above their heads as Seb points a *gun* at them.

"Seb," I say, scared of the look in his eyes. "What are you doing?"

The girls watch Seb, their eyes on the weapon. I touch Seb's shoulder lightly. I need him to look at me, to break the spell.

"They were spying on us," he says. His voice is high, almost hysterical.

"Don't be crazy, Seb. They're Sanctuary. It's obvious."

They're wearing the same greens and yellows as Noah, bows on their backs. One of the twins has short white hair and the other has shoulder-length white hair. "Just lower the gun. Come on. At least let them speak."

But the girls look amused, not scared.

"No!" Seb barks.

A rustle of footsteps at my back. Noah moves past me, and too fast for me to follow, he has kicked Seb hard in the back of one knee, whilst simultaneously snatching the gun out of his hand. Seb goes down and Noah sits on him, locking Seb's arms behind his back and shoving the gun into the belt of his trousers.

"What the hell were you doing?" he rages. "They're our friends!"

Seb stops struggling and Noah lets him go. He slides off his back, and pulls Seb roughly to his knees.

"This guy is trouble," the short-haired twin says. "You're sure he's Giften?"

"He's not Giften, Alia," says Noah, sighing.

The twins glance at each other. The twin with longer hair starts to shake her head.

"You brought a *non* here to kill us?" she says. "Have you gone crazy?"

"Take it down a gregious notch," hisses Noah. "They're not our enemies. They're just scared. They've lived in one community their whole lives. They don't know anything about anything. Never mind two white-haired witches creeping about in the dark."

"Hey," I say. "We're here, aren't we? We can't be that useless!"

"Why didn't you two just announce yourselves?" Noah asks the twins. "Annis?"

"For the love of the land, Noah. How in hell were we to know you weren't *their* prisoner?" she says.

The twins move towards me as Stace and Scottie come into the clearing. They lift their bows from their shoulders, but make no move to load arrows.

"Because," Noah points to Scottie who is cowering behind Stace, "I was happily shooting arrows with the kid. Did I look like a prisoner? Anyway, they're coming back with us to the Island tomorrow," he says. "Even this one." He gestures at Seb with his thumb.

The twins start to laugh. They laugh for a long time.

"It's not funny," I snap, finally. "He made a mistake, that's all. Seb, tell them you made a mistake."

But Seb stays silent, still on his knees, eyes on the ground.

"We won't kill him, OK? And you, Noah, will have to tell Zan exactly what you're doing with a bunch of nons at Cove's Bay," says Alia.

"*They're* Giften." Noah points at me and Scottie, but Scottie won't come out from behind Stace.

"You need to start talking," Annis says.

Seb gets to his feet. It's almost completely dark, but I think I hear shame in his voice.

"I'm sorry," he says. "I was scared." Is it shame?

I take out my wind-up torch and shine it into his face.

He blinks in the light. "I panicked. I wanted to protect my friends. I saw you with the binos. You were hiding and… and watching us." He speaks fast as he recounts his side of the story. He doesn't need to convince anyone, though. It's obvious what happened. He was startled, and after Graylings, who can blame him for being a bit jumpy?

"He has a point," Noah says. "But let's move on, OK? We have to talk."

The twins exchange a glance and smirk. They are so confident, so strange. I find myself liking them, even though they seem to hate nons.

"Listen," Alia says to Seb, ignoring Noah. "We'll let this go because Noah says you're all right. He's an idiot, but not a bad judge of character." She makes the shape of a gun with her fingers and fires at Seb. "But you're not getting that weapon back."

Seb grins. "I don't know how to use it anyway," he says, ducking Alia's imaginary bullet.

Annis nudges her sister. "Enough. They're not our friends." She looks at Noah. "They're not coming to the Island, understood?" And then she gestures at me, "Push it and your Giften won't be coming either."

"They are coming," Noah insists. "And I'll tell you why if you let me." But the twins are stony-faced, united in their rejection. I flick off my torch and we stand in the cold blue light of the moon.

"I'm Ruthie," I say. "I think you know my dad. His name is Dan. He saves Giften."

15

Life in a community isn't simple; you worry about your kids, the weather, this year's harvest. We have only one thing to think about: we rescue Giften. If we're lucky enough to find a MAG or two on the road, we deal with them too. We're focused. Mixing our lives with yours, staying in one place, making friends with nons? In no time we'd be worrying on who is and isn't pulling their weight come harvest time. And to hell with the Giften.

ESHE, SANCTUARY

athered around a small fire we talked into the night. I told the twins about Graylings, about the Circle, about Dad. We told them of the Circle's plans to attack the Base, to free the City and the North of MAGs for ever. They asked question after insistent question until they ran out and stopped talking altogether. Their eyes on the flames, the twins sat in silence. Gone was the confidence, and in its place a kind of sadness. They had picked up Giften from Graylings in the past. They knew Salvage Sam. In those long minutes, with only the distant sound of waves splashing onto the shore, part of me hoped they would refuse, once more, to take us to the Island.

Seb and Stace and I would head for the City, find Dev and, with the Circle, we'd make a plan to rescue Dad. This was better, I decided, feeling a little buoyed. I didn't want to tell the story of Graylings, of Dad's ambush again and again to the Sanctuary. I didn't want to leave the mainland at all.

"Zan needs to hear this," sighed Annis finally.

My heart sank and kept on sinking until Stace reached across and squeezed my shoulder. *One step at a time*, her eyes told me. *We made a promise; we have a job to do.* I had to admit that I didn't much like the idea of telling Ian that we never even made it onto the Island.

"She does," Alia said, "so it's down to you, Noah. You explain everything to her, the second we land. Don't give her a chance to get all het up about the others. The nons."

Noah didn't answer and instead looked at me. The fire was dying and we were all tired. I wished I was already asleep.

"What?" I said. In the firelight he looked older, like a man. But then he grinned and the dip in his cheek appeared. He was just a boy.

"Ruthie will tell her. She convinced you, didn't she?"

*   *   *

At first light, we drive, in silence, down to the sea. Annis and Alia are squashed in the back of the solar with me, Stace and Scottie. It's uncomfortable, but there's a tension in the car that's even more irksome. The Giften are worried about what lies ahead, about their leader who has no time for *outsiders*. At last, at the foot of the hill, on grassy sand, Noah pulls over and we all stagger out. He parks the car in a tangle of brambles, alongside three other solars; Sanctuary solars.

It's early and there's no sign of the sun. A grey blanket of cloud hovers over the grey blanket of the sea. A fierce wind is blowing inland and the boat, moored to a pole lashed to boulders further along the beach, bucks and sways on the lapping waves a short distance from the beach. I assume that any minute one of the twins will decide it's too rough to cross. That we should wait a little longer. As the first drops of rain begin to thud out of the sky, the twins haul a small rubber dinghy out of the bushes by the solars. Nothing is going to stop them. Certainly not a bit of rain and wind. I hold on tightly to the sides of the dinghy as it ploughs through the water and shut my eyes. In seconds I'm bitterly cold as the small boat bucks the shallow waves, sending sea spray into my face and down my neck. In two trips we're all on board and the dinghy is hitched to the back of the boat. Alia starts the motor and I take a final look at the hills where we camped last night; the next time I see them I will be alone with my friends or we will have persuaded the Sanctuary to join us. Right now, I have no idea which it will be.

Alia's mouth is a thin line as she steers us towards Foundation Island. The wind doesn't let up, but the clouds begin to disperse, just a little, as the sun peeks over the lip of the horizon, a half ball of yellow light. The sea is the colour of melted boulders. A salty, sour smell fills the air and the wind whips tears from my eyes. The engine hums as Alia turns the wheel.

The rest of us huddle for warmth on a long wooden bench. Each dip and rise in the water takes us ever closer to the blob of green in the distance.

*   *   *

The Island comes into view through the sea mist. High above the water, dense woodland reaches for the sky. There is a small bay where another boat sits, half in half out of the water, on stubby grass. On the headland above the bay, a lone figure with binos peers out to sea.

"It's Zan," shouts Alia into the wind. "You guys ready?" She's looking at me, so I nod even though I'm not, and watch Zan track down the hill to the bay as the front of the boat bumps land and halts.

Through her thin shirt I see muscly arms, a strong back, a flat lean stomach. Her skin is a tone lighter than mine. I notice that her eyes, as they sweep over our faces, are the colour of amber. Zan's hair hangs in light brown dreadlocks down her back.

Noah throws out a rope which she catches, but doesn't

move to tie it to the post in the sand. Stace's hand slips into mine.

"Wait," says Zan. "Who are these three? I thought it was just the Graylings boy." She is more than ready to turn us around. I want to scream, *I don't even want to be here.*

"This is Ruthie," Noah says, steadily. He lays a hand on my shoulder. I want to shake him off, but I don't move. "She's Giften and yes, that's the Graylings kid." Noah grins at Scottie, but the little boy just looks scared.

"And those two? Tell me they're not nons, Noah." Zan's hands are on her hips.

The boat tilts and sways in the shallows; Noah catches my arm as I almost lose my footing.

"They just want to talk to you, Zan," he says.

"Gregor!" Zan yells up the hill.

Almost immediately, a *giant* appears at the top of the hill. With his black hair and beard, he could be Owen's brother. Even Seb does a double-take. Gregor pounds down the rocky path. Two angry Sanctuary, I think. And then I want to laugh, I haven't said even one word and she's about to set this ogre on us.

"Zan, you don't need Gregor. This isn't an ambush. For the love of the land, just hear them out," Noah says as Gregor steps onto the grass.

"Hey, Noah." Gregor is grinning widely. He isn't an ogre at all. His eyes are kind and curious. He waves at Scottie with his fingers; Scottie stares at him, open-mouthed. "This the Graylings kid? Wow, you've been busy, all these Giften. Welcome!" he booms, spreading his arms wide and then, when no one responds, his arms fall to his sides and he turns to Zan, looking puzzled. "You OK, Zan?"

"They're not *all* Giften!" she snaps. "Just two of them. So *two of them* can stay, or they can *all* go." She gestures at the twins, who haven't moved or said a word since we landed. "See that Noah takes them back. And whoever you people are, forget you ever came here. No *nons* on the Island, I don't care what your story is." With that, Zan heads back up the hill.

It's over, I think. And I'm glad. I can't *make* her talk to us. But then Dev's voice is in my ear, and the image of turning this boat around and heading back to the mainland suddenly feels like surrender. *You're a fighter, Ruthie. So fight for this.*

"We'll go," I call out to Zan's retreating back. "Maybe we made a mistake about you." She is still walking away, and I feel a bubble of anger. "The MAGs just murdered a whole community for its Giften, but if you don't care then you're right, it's best we leave!"

Halfway up the slope, Zan stops and slowly turns around.

I draw Scottie to my side. The words come easily now. "They killed everyone at Graylings just because they couldn't find this boy."

"That's right, Zan," says Noah. "Everyone's dead."

"Apart from me," says Scottie in a whisper. I pull him closer. "Mum made me run. The MAGs did catch me, but I got away when they were peeing, and then Noah got me out of the bushes." He rolls up his sleeves and Zan comes back. She steps into the boat, and is smiling at Scottie as she takes his thin arms in her hands.

"We have a doc here who will take care of your scratches. OK?"

Scottie nods slowly. He has melted a little of her ice.

"Graylings is gone?" Zan is looking at Noah.

Gregor's head dips to his chest. He squeezes his hands into fists.

"I was on my way to pick up Scottie here when I met some Circle," Noah explains. "They were meeting Ruthie's dad at Graylings, but he never made it. MAG ambush." He pauses. "His name is Dan."

"Dan?" Zan's eyes go wide, and she finally looks at me. "Our contact, Dan? He's your father?"

I nod.

It's raining. The wind is up, sharp and abrasive. It feels like it's ripping the skin off my face, but no one moves.

"What do you want from us?" Zan asks me.

So I tell her.

*   *   *

Old tents, showing years of wear and repair, are set up in a clearing above the bay where the two Sanctuary boats are now moored. I dig another sweater out of my bag. I can't remember ever feeling warm.

In the centre of the clearing are the damp remains of a huge fire, charred logs steam at the edges. Clusters of silver birch overhang the camp, their dripping leaves shine autumn yellow. The land beyond the clearing is a wilderness of shrubs and bushes, jostling one another for space, and beyond is the dense, vibrant green woodland I had watched grow in size on our approach.

Down in the bay, after I'd told Zan the whole story, we were led up here. Young men and women emerge from the woods and from tents. Maybe twenty of them, give or take. Smiling, curious faces surround us. They wear the same patchwork clothes of muted colours as Noah, and finally I understand why. The faded greens, yellows and greys are camouflage. Some of the younger men and women have rings of silver in their noses, their ears.

"Get this fire going, Annis." Zan appears from the woodland, a tall, striking woman by her side, who looks at the three of us with contempt. "And then everyone with me." She doesn't mean us. Zan heads into a large square tent, followed by the rest of the Sanctuary.

Stace, Seb, Scottie and I stand in front of the spark-ing fire, our hands held out for warmth. A chill has gone straight through my double layer of sweaters and into my bones. Only one thing will make me feel better. Whatever is going to happen is out of my hands now. I have told Zan our story, asked for her help. The Sanctuary must decide.

"Wanna make mud?" I ask Scottie.

On our knees at the edge of the camp, we scrabble through a layer of weeds to reveal the soil. I close my eyes and feel a trickle of warmth spread up my arms into my chest and down into my body. I dig deeper, sensing a new vibration—is it the sea? Or is it the presence of so many Giften in one place? I think of the pulpy, brown apple, shrivelled by my touch, in the orchard; if I can enjoy the warmth of the earth, maybe my gift is OK.

"Ruthie, are you ready?" Noah hovers over us.

I feel as though I've been caught doing something I shouldn't. He smiles. His eyes are the exact colour of the sea. I open my mouth to tell him but catch myself in time.

Scottie and I fling the earth from our fingers. Noah reaches for a clay bottle on the ground and pours a stream of water over my hands.

"Now me," Scottie says, showing us filthy palms.

"Zan's not happy," Noah says, looking out to sea. "I tried to warn Ian."

I turn to look at the clearing; the Giften have gathered around the fire, standing about or sitting on tree stumps. The rain has stopped, but the sky is still grey. I'm warmer now, ready for Zan's pronouncement. Flames fly from the fire and flicker out. None of the Giften are smiling.

Zan is on her feet, her back to the blaze. She looms over us as we take a stump each. She's maybe a little older than Mum, and she's staring at me just like Mum does before she tells me off. For the second time this morning I have the crazy impulse to laugh.

"I'm sorry about Dan," she says. "I'm sorry about Graylings. But this… this partnership with the Circle, it can't happen. We are not friends of the Circle, we—"

"Damn right!" a voice shouts. A tall woman whose hair is woven into a series of tiny plaits which lie in thin neat rows over her scalp, is on her feet, skirting the edge of the fire until she's face to face with Zan. She's vibrating with anger. Her hand rests on the hilt of a long, sheathed knife in her belt.

"Who *are* these kids? What are they doing here?" Her skin is a deeper brown than mine. She has a pale brown scar down one cheek and wears the purple sash of a medic. Doc Pam doesn't carry a knife, I think idly.

"Eshe!" Zan snaps, taking her arm. Everyone in the circle startles. "I told you this isn't how we're going to do this. I told you I would talk to them. I told you—"

"*You told me, you told me,*" spits Eshe. She shakes Zan off, taking a step back. Five Giften rise to their feet and move to stand behind Eshe. "You're supposed to be our *leader*, but you allow these strangers on to the Island. You allow them to tell us we have to go to the City, join the gregious *Circle* for the love of the land, and fight *their* wars."

"It's not *their* war, Eshe," Noah's steady voice, from the other side of the clearing.

"The Circle is not our people!" Eshe cuts in. "Their blood hunger, their chaos *kills* our people." Her voice drops when she says, "Ravelston Road. Have you forgotten so soon, Noah?"

"It's in the past," Noah says. He doesn't move from his log, he doesn't raise his voice. "If we keep looking behind us we're bound to fall over sooner or later."

"Fifty Giften! I'm supposed to forget about *fifty* of our people." Her eyes flash as she rounds on Zan. "Blown apart by explosives alongside filthy MAGs."

"The Circle didn't *know*." Noah is on his feet now. The Giften around Eshe close ranks, barring his way. "What's this?" he says waving at them. "Your protection?"

"Eshe! Stand down!" yells Zan as Gregor moves to her side.

But Eshe and the Giften hold their ground.

"This is a chance to get rid of the MAGs for ever." And then I'm on my feet too. When you have nothing to lose by having a go, have a go, I decide. "The Circle is going to fight anyway. But we… *you*, could make the difference between winning and losing."

"The Circle is reckless," Zan says. "We can't risk our lives for them. The wound is too deep."

"Only because you keep poking it," I say. Zan takes a step forward and I back into my stump and stumble. "Noah, you met Ian." I feel desperate now. "Tell them what he said about *history*, about the *future*, a new future." I want to win them over; I want my words to be as powerful as Eshe's, as steady as Zan's, but the faces of the Giften remain impassive. Whatever happened to the Sanctuary on the Ravelston Road is a fire they stoke every day.

"Leave it, Ruthie. She knows. You already told her, remember? Zan has decided," Noah says, turning to walk away. "I'll take you back to your solar tomorrow." He exits the clearing and disappears into one of the ramshackle tents.

"Scottie can stay," Zan says. "So can you, Ruthie. But your friends must go."

"You didn't see Graylings, Zan," I say quietly. "None of you did. You didn't see what they did to those people. You might ambush the MAGs on the roads, take their solars, rescue Giften, but it's not enough. It's no longer enough."

"I'm sorry, Ruthie. My word is final," she says.

16

*It's hard to believe in evil when you wake up to the
sun breathing life into the crops. It should be enough.
But Saige Corentin put a price on our survival, our
happiness, when she targeted the Giften. If anyone
started a war, it was her. Logan, listen to me, I'd
give my life to stop her. And so would you.*

DAN, THE FIELD

"How in the hell are we going to get to the City?"
Stace says after the Giften have dispersed from
the clearing. She's on her feet, pacing up and
down, brushing sparks from the leaping fire from her
clothes. Her long black hair flies in ribbons in the wind.
She pulls a woollen length from a pocket and fixes her
hair into a high ponytail. Her face is pinched red by
the cold.

Seb is staring into the flames. "I don't know why you
think that's a good idea," he says. "None of us can fight,
not like Dev."

They've both moved on already. *Zan has decided*, Noah
said, and now… now what? The way Seb is sitting, the

deep gloom in his voice, releases something inside me, an urge to scream at him to wake up. I need to move on too.

"*We* can do it, Stace," I say tightly, on my feet now, pacing. "We can take it slow. Drive in the dark. We've got Dad's map. We... we—"

Seb catches my arm and spins me around to face him. Now *he's* angry too.

"Don't worry, Seb!" I say, yanking free. "Your promise to me, to keep me safe? I'm good, OK? I release you."

"It's not that simple though, is it, Ruthie?" he says, rising from his stump. "What kind of man leaves two girls to go charging into war with the Circle?"

My anger vanishes and I snort. But Stace is already laughing.

"You can't stop us, Seb." Her arms are folded tight over her chest. "You either come with us and shut up about being a gregious *man* or you make your own way back to the Field."

*　　　*　　　*

Inside our musty tent, Stace is dozing. I lie beside her, wide awake. It's been a tough few hours since we left the mainland and I yearn to blot it all out with sleep, but I can't stop the whirring in my head. We're only fifteen years old; can we really do this? Mum's face flashes in front of my eyes. I know what she'd say. Come home. Come back to the Field. Wind batters the tent, loud, insistent. How does anyone ever sleep on this island? I block out thoughts of Mum. They don't help.

Footsteps outside, lots of them, running.

"Boat coming in!" the voices call.

My hands start to throb. They said MAGs don't come to the Island, but the MAGs never used to wipe out entire communities either.

In the late afternoon light, Stace and I follow the Giften, racing down the hillside to the bay. Seb is already there, standing with the twins. When he sees us, Noah moves through the small crowd until he's beside me. Scottie hangs on to his coat, his face pale and fearful. I take his small hand in mine.

"OK, kid?" He nods and shivers and I draw him closer. "Who is it?" I ask. It's not MAGs because not a single Giften has drawn their bow. The relief is huge.

"Not Saige Corentin. Don't worry." Noah is probably eighteen, like Seb, but he seems older. Ever since I first laid eyes on it, I have had the strange urge to touch my finger to the hole in his cheek. The urge comes again because he's grinning. I look away.

The clouds are clearing; patches of blue sky appear between the grey. The sun, a glowing orange ball, hovers over the horizon. A single figure ploughs the waves with long oars.

"Damn fool is rowing!" Zan shouts, laughing. She turns to me, her face a wide smile. "It's Logan."

For a moment I don't understand. Logan? The Recorder is coming to the Island?

"Ruthie, you should think about staying here. With us." Noah raises his eyebrows as though he's asking a question, and then he reaches for me. For a mad moment I think he's going to grab me, tell me to come to my senses, that I'm just a girl not a warrior, but his fingers plunge into my messy curls. I jerk away and his hand falls.

"Sorry. I-I- Your curls, they're so... I..." His face is as red as mine.

Stace, over his shoulder, is grinning and behind her, Seb isn't.

"We've decided to go the City," I tell him. "First thing tomorrow. I wish we'd never come here." I'm about to say more, but then Logan, ruddy-cheeked and frowning, makes an announcement.

"I have news," the Recorder tells Zan. "It's bad. The very worst."

The rain starts to come down in gusting sheets as Zan and Logan lead the way up the hillside back to camp. Zan heads for the large tent and everyone follows. Logan brings bad news. My heart is pounding. Both Stace and Seb look scared. We share one thought, one unbearable thought. Has something happened to the Field?

A ground mat covers the earth and a small wood-burning stove takes the chill out of the air; its stove pipe juts through a neat hole in the canvas. The floor is littered with patchwork cushions and rag rugs, but no one sits.

Low murmurs fill the room while we wait. Logan, Zan and Gregor huddle at the front of the tent, talking in low voices. I watch Zan start to tug on her dreads; her face falls as she listens to the Recorder. Her eyes move from Logan's face and stare, unseeing, at the Giften amassing around them. Gregor rubs her back, whispers in her ear.

"Listen up," Zan says, clearing her throat.

The murmuring stops. I ready myself to hear the *very worst*.

"Ottoway is down," Zan says. She glances at Gregor, and takes a deep breath. "Whatever happened at Graylings has happened again. They wouldn't give up their Giften. This is no longer just the Circle's problem. It's all of ours." She pauses, her eyes sweeping over our faces. "I say we fight!"

For a moment I feel like I might faint, the relief is so strong. My family is alive. The Field is alive.

Movement in the crowd, voices rising, cursing the MAGs. Logan meets my eyes and there is something in them I recognize, something I need to remember about myself. Determination; the Recorder looks set on a course from which there is no turning back.

From the back of the room Eshe's voice is louder than anyone else's. "Ottoway is *your* community, Zan!" she shouts, moving through the room. "You want to use us to take *your* revenge."

Zan's community? And then it comes to me. *Zan* is *Xandria*, from Ottoway.

"Eshe!" Zan holds up a palm as she approaches. "The last time I checked *I* was leader of the Sanctuary. Not you."

"Stand down, Eshe," says a voice from the floor, and then others.

"Let Zan speak."

"Let her speak."

Eshe's five followers draw closer; three women and two men.

"Cut it out," booms Gregor. "We are not fighting amongst ourselves."

"Yes we are!" hisses Eshe, jabbing a finger at Zan. "If she makes this personal, we *are* fighting amongst ourselves."

"You'll have your turn, Eshe. I want to hear her out," Noah says, moving to Zan's side.

"Little boy with big words." Eshe looks like she's going to say more, but then she turns on her heel, and with her team, she heads to the back of the tent to stand by the flapping canvas door.

"Eshe's right," Zan calls above the muttering voices. "Ottoway *was* my community. But its loss is much, much more than *personal*. Now, the time has come for us to reach beyond our borders. The communities are losing their lives to protect the Giften, they suffer for *us*. We are the Sanctuary, but we are also the sons and daughters of our communities."

"You're a leaf twisting in the wind," calls Eshe from the back of the room. "What kind of leader changes her mind like this? And you, Logan. When did you become a mouthpiece for the Circle?"

I don't know what she means for a moment, but then it falls into place. Why would Logan bring this news here unless it had been made clear that it was exactly what the Sanctuary needed to hear right now? News so bad it would convince old enemies to join forces.

"The kind of leader who isn't afraid of what you think of her," Gregor says. "The kind of leader who is brave enough to take a gregious minute and look at what's going on." He points at Logan. "The Recorder has brought news, another community is dead. How many more must die before we step up? How many must die for us?"

It starts slowly, a low hum in the room, voices saying, *We'll fight* and *Let's go* and *Gregor's right*. And then it builds until feet are stomping and hands are clapping.

Stace is shouting too. She turns to me, her eyes bright in the gloom. "We did it, Ruthie!"

A gust of wind rips through the tent, as Eshe pulls aside the canvas flap. "I don't want to be part of this, Zan. Fighting a war that's not ours? That isn't us." Eshe's eyes blaze. She looks at me, at Stace. "These people, who are they? Children playing at war."

"I'm not a kid," I say. "I made it here, didn't I?" I sound petulant, defensive, just like a kid, but Eshe's attention has already shifted back to Zan.

"We're going up country and I'm taking a boat. If you want it back, send someone with us."

"Don't do this," says Gregor. "Eshe, stay. Talk to me."

But she's already gone.

Eshe and her five followers leave straight after the meeting, pausing only to grab their stuff from their tents, the wounds of an old injustice still too fresh to ignore. Zan keeps her distance, watching as they make their way down the path to the inlet, Noah on their heels, tasked by Zan to bring the boat back once they are safely on the mainland.

*   *   *

Flaming torches are planted at the edges of the camp clearing. The fire is stoked back to life and glows orange and yellow and white in the gathering dusk. The Giften move around in silence, making soup on another fire, slicing bread, handing round bowls.

Zan didn't ask Logan where the two canvas bags of guns came from as they were hauled from the boat onto land, but I can guess who handed them over.

"We leave for the City tomorrow," says Zan. Her eyes are glassy. She's been crying for her people, her blood people. But there's also strength in her voice. I realize she has put aside the dead of Ravelston Road to save the living.

On stumps we have dragged closer to the fire, drinking soup from wooden bowls, we listen as Zan circles the clearing, stopping to talk to the Giften, asking for their thoughts. They greet her with eager faces and serious words.

"It'll be dark soon, so I'm sending some of you to the mainland tonight." Zan points out six Giften who nod their heads. "Gather the Sanctuary. Check the Tombs are secure. We'll be with you as soon as we can."

The Tombs: a Sanctuary safe house in the City. *Stinky, dark underground rooms.* Big enough to hold two hundred Giften.

"Gather the Sanctuary?" I ask the twins. "I thought you were nomadic, spread out all over the country?"

"Most of us are in and around the City right now, which is lucky. Otherwise it would have taken days and days to get everyone back," Alia tells me. "They're waiting for us to come off the Island. We were set to head up country, hoping to pounce on a few MAG convoys ourselves." She looks into the fire. "Save a few communities from making the harvest Offering."

"You will be spared from having to make these random attacks, now that you have decided to join the fight," says Logan, seated beside Seb.

I notice the hem of Logan's coat, wet and filthy; something catches in my chest and I reach across Seb for the Recorder's hand, and squeeze. I'm offered a smile, but it doesn't reach Logan's eyes.

Zan takes a deep breath. "We will invite the Circle to meet with us." Her tone is unwavering, unlike the light in her eyes, which looks like it's gone out. Flames from the fire dance in the growing dark, throwing yellow streaks into the clearing. She starts to speak, and the Giften voices join her chant, "*We live in the shadows. We are nomadic. We are the Sanctuary.*"

Seb hasn't spoken a word since the meeting in the tent. I nudge him.

"Are you good?" I say.

He nods slowly, staring into his full bowl of soup. "I'll go wherever you want to go, Ruthie," he says.

Instead of resolve I hear resignation in his voice. But maybe I'm wrong.

"To the Tombs!" Noah appears in front of us, back from his trip to the mainland with Eshe. He drains his bowl and drags a sleeve across his mouth. He nods towards Logan, who is talking with Zan at the edge of the clearing. "Didn't know our Recorder was Circle," he says.

17

I don't know how to think about the Burn. As a Giften I grow food. My touch is restorative to the land, drawing out nutrients and moisture. But the Burn moves faster. Fruit ripens, flowers open, a seed bursts, but you can't control it, it carries on until the fruit or plant is dead, ashes. And if you're angry, stay away from people—unless you want to hurt them, of course.

ZAN, SANCTUARY

'll be glad to get off this Island," Gregor's voice booms from the clearing early the next morning. "I want to get dry at least once before I die." He's the only one who laughs.

I nudge Stace awake. Her hair is a black mask over her face, and minutes later we're dressed, ready to step outside. Tomorrow we'll be in the Tombs and my life will be even stranger than it is today. I imagine the Giften meeting the Circle for the first time. Could it work? Or will they kill each other?

"You know, Ruthie," Stace says, catching my arm before I draw aside the tent flaps. "What do you think

Mum and Dad would say if they knew we're hanging out with the Sanctuary, about to join forces with Circle to launch an attack on the Base?" She's smiling, her cheeks are rosy from sleep.

I wonder what it must be like to be Stace. To live without a secret so dangerous that it risks the lives of everyone you know and love. "You say it like it's a great adventure," I say meanly.

"Come on. A few days ago we had normal lives doing normal things. And now, now we're *here*."

"But I'm not *normal* though, am I?" I snap, holding up my hands.

But she pushes them aside. "Keep telling yourself that," she says. "You know what? I think you feel just like me, just as mixed up about growing old in the Field as I am. You use that gift to stop you wanting more."

Her words seem to reach me from a long way away. I'm dizzy, unmoored. I think about Dad staying away when he could have come back. I think about Mum *moving on* with Owen, and I wonder which one of them I'm like. It seems obvious to Stace, but not to me. I shake away the thoughts and exit the tent.

The camp is in motion when I step outside into the dawn air. It's cool and a light breeze blows in off the sea, flinging last night's rain off the trees. The sun on the horizon is a milky red, cloaked behind an invisible mist. In the clearing, the twins fill clay bottles with leftover soup and fresh water, while Seb deposits apples and pears from two large piles into a line of backpacks propped against tree stumps around the glowing embers of last night's fire. Scottie trails Noah and Gregor as they seal the bedding and tents into huge canvas bags and go back and forth to a storage hut in the woods.

"What can I do?" I ask Noah as he begins another trip. He drops a heavy bag and Gregor picks it up, hoisting it onto a free shoulder.

"Don't worry, Noah," Gregor grunts, as he heads into the woods. "I can take yours. You chat with Ruthie."

Scottie stands between the two men, unsure of who to follow.

Noah gives him a gentle shove. "Go with Gregor, Scottie. I'll catch up."

I catch Stace's eye as she emerges from the tent and my stomach clenches, letting out a deep rumble.

"You OK?" Noah hands me a pear from one of the fruit piles.

I take an angry bite. His eyes, grey, bright and friendly, peer into mine. His shirt clings to his chest and tummy in damp folds. He's been hard at work while I've been sleeping.

"I'm fine," I say. "You?"

"You sure? You seem—"

"I said I'm fine!" I snap.

"You're not." Stace stands before us, her hands plunged deep into the pockets of her patchwork waterproof. "And it's my fault. I'm sorry." But she doesn't sound sorry.

"It's so easy for you, Stace," I say.

Noah looks confused. He glances at Stace, then back at me, opens his mouth, but this is nothing to do with him, so I plough on.

"It's simple, get out of the Field and have a new life. An exciting life—whatever it takes. But I had no choice." Seb appears at Stace's shoulder. He looks as puzzled as Noah. "So *I'm sorry* if I'm not having fun." Dad is missing and the Field is in danger; all the communities are in danger. Because of people like me.

But Stace is no longer looking at me, she's staring at my pear; shrivelled into a black, stringy mess in my fist. It's happening again. A humming fills my head, I feel dizzy, embarrassed, the Island falls away. And then a faraway voice breaks the spell, *Logan's* voice, saying, *It's OK, Ruthie. You're OK*. But I can't take my eyes off the revolting mess. A sudden heat fills my face as a hush falls over the clearing. The twins approach, serious, unsmiling. I fling the desiccated remains onto the ground, stamp on them with my boot. My cheeks are burning.

"Zan," Alia shouts, towards the bay, where Zan and Gregor are checking over the boats.

My heart sinks even deeper into my chest. Is this the moment Zan decides she doesn't want any broken Giften around her precious Sanctuary?

"You don't need to be scared, Ruthie," Annis says, her hand on my shoulder. "This is a *thing*. It's rare, but it's part of the gift for some of us. *Burning*," she whispers.

Over her shoulder I watch Zan approach. Annis points to the pear, tilts her chin at me.

"So," Zan says, "you've done this before?"

I nod. "Once," I say.

Zan comes closer, I smell woodsmoke on her clothes, in her hair. She lays her hands on my shoulders. "You're scared, right?" But I don't say anything. She lets go of me and plucks a few blue wildflowers from the edge of the clearing. They lie still in her palm while her face changes. Her eyes narrow in concentration. Tiny petals stretch and open wide. "Keep watching," she says, her voice suddenly gruff. The flowers close and begin to shrink, they become brown and then black and then ashes. Zan shakes her hand and ashes rise into the air. "If I touch you when I'm angry I could hurt you."

"You're still Giften though?" I say fast, my breath catching in my throat. "You can still grow?"

"Of course," she says, grinning widely. Rain mists the clearing, tiny drops of light falling from the sky into the hissing fire. They land in Zan's hair, on her eyelashes. I look at my hands, grubby with the remains of a shrivelled pear, but they're still Giften hands.

"Have you hurt anyone?" The question that I buried so deep I didn't know I was about to speak it until I heard the words come out of my mouth.

Zan grins. "Only MAGs who get in my way. The first time it happened I didn't know what I was doing. Big guy he was, on top of me, hands around my neck." She raises her hands to close around the invisible arms of a murderous MAG. "And he just crumpled on top of me."

"You killed him?" Stace asks. Her hands go to her own throat as if she's afraid Zan will burn her next.

"No!" Zan laughs. "I just hurt him. To kill him I had to use an arrow."

I stare at my hands again, my fingers. I flex them and make fists. This is bad. I don't understand why Zan is so happy. Bile rises in my throat. How long before I hurt someone who's innocent?

"What if I do it by accident?" I ask, plunging my hands into the depths of my trouser pockets. The sweet face of Ant flashes in my mind. Mum.

Zan nods at Gregor who pulls up his sleeve to reveal a patch of hairless, wrinkled, deep brown skin on his arm.

"She didn't mean to," he says. "We know to keep our distance if she's angry."

"Thank God Eshe can't do it," says Noah.

The twins snort.

"Not funny, Noah," says Zan. "Ruthie, if you need to be angry when you're not, like I was just now with the flowers, use a memory." But she can see it's too soon to teach me about the wonders of the Burn. She touches my shoulder and I meet her twinkling amber eyes. "It's OK. You'll see."

The Giften disperse, but Stace and Noah and Seb linger.

"I'm fine," I tell them, sullenly. "Really." I begin to reason that if Zan, the leader of the Sanctuary, can do it, then perhaps it isn't the curse I'm imagining. "Let's just get on with packing up."

"Listen," Noah says softly, as the others walk away. "I know that was weird." He takes a step closer. "But it might be useful in the City."

His words scare me. He's looking at me as if he's waiting for a light to go on in my eyes. *Yes, that's just what I needed to hear. I can burn MAGs and save the world.*

"I have something for you." He reaches into a trouser pocket and pulls out a thin bracelet of tiny opaque blue stones. "I don't know what the gems are," he says, placing the bracelet in my hand. I look at the stones so I don't have to look at him. A lump in my throat.

"Thanks," I say. To my embarrassment the lump expands to block any other words coming out. I turn away.

"I found it in the City, a long time ago. I've just been carrying it around. It doesn't really suit me." He smiles and I find I'm smiling too. But then I think of Dad, the MAGs dragging him away. This small act of kindness has undone me.

"Ruthie," he says, "this bracelet doesn't have to mean anything. You're sad, that's all, and it's pretty."

He picks up another canvas bag, throws it over his shoulder and heads for the woods.

"You're pretty too," he calls back.

I glance up to catch Seb looking away quickly; he heard everything. I shove the bracelet into my pocket.

PART THREE

The City

I was a smallie at the time; I didn't know that monsters look just like the rest of us. She arrived with her 'team' as she called them. They studied the soil, took some back with them to the South. When she came again she wanted to take Janice, the Giften girl. We said no, but they took her anyway. Never saw her again. I never saw Saige Corentin again either, but she's here, in the City. Her new team are the MAGs, I guess. And now she has her pick of Giften.

PETER, BOW'S FARM

18

I first came to the North many years ago. As you well know, the Darkening, with its flooding, storms, earthquakes and a civil war, separated the North from the South, and your land became a grand experiment in isolation. Two hundred years later I joined an expedition to find out how the land had thrived without the pollutants of man and machine. Abandoned for so long, we believed it was devoid of human life. We never expected much of anything. Instead we found miracles.

SAIGE, THE CITY

The mainland feels more solid than the Island, like we're back in the real world. But it's still there, in the distance, a green boulder in the grey sea. Uninhabited for the single hour it took to cross the water. Two Giften will take the boats back to the Island and sit out what's coming, and for just a moment, as I watch them sail away, I wish I was with them.

I stare up at the bouldered hillside where Seb pointed a gun at the Giften twins, a lifetime ago. We haven't returned empty-handed after all. The Sanctuary, for a while at least, is here, ready to talk and maybe to fight. And I have a new gift.

Twelve of us trek up the rocky path from the beach to find four cars, including Logan's yellow solar, hidden from the track by clusters of bramble and thistle.

The Recorder is solemn as we say goodbye, wishing me luck, hugging Stace, shaking hands with Seb. There is no tearful farewell. I recall Logan's last visit to the Field, when we entered the Clearing to find Dad with Old Pete. *Talk in a bit?* Dad had asked. It's obvious now; Logan was already deep into the resistance.

"With me, Ruthie," Zan calls, climbing into one of the solars. "Nicely charged," she says, clicking on the engine.

Stace is up front, itching to map read, folding and unfolding Gregor's sheet of neatly drawn lines.

"I know the way." Zan grins and Stace tucks away the map.

Scottie is curled against me, almost asleep before the journey has even begun; Seb takes the boy's hand. The beach, the sea and the Island fall away as Zan ploughs through the thistle onto a steep track. The sun emerges just as we reach the top. She pauses here for a moment and our heads turn towards the shimmering blue water, not a cloud in the sky, Foundation Island, a small green oasis in the distance, and two tiny boats bobbing their way home.

"*Now* it's sunny?" says Stace.

"It's probably still raining on the Island though," Zan says with a sigh, and our convoy of three solars and their passengers begins the journey south and to the City.

*   *   *

A week ago I'd never even seen a large expanse of water, and now I've sailed on the sea and spent one night on an island. As we head towards the Bridge, I try and picture what a road across the sea might look like.

"We need to be ready," Zan announces. "Remember, if MAGs come our way, we stick to the story."

We're part of a community travelling to the City, starved off our land and hoping for shelter and the benevolence of the MAGs. That's *the story*.

By mid-morning, sunshine pounds the solar. Sweat traces lines down Zan's cheeks, her neck. Scottie is still asleep, his cheek stuck to my bare arm.

"He's sleeping all the time," Seb says softly, stroking the boy's damp forehead.

"Are you surprised?" I ask. "He's lost *everyone*."

"I'm not surprised he's in shock, poor kid. I'm surprised you think the City is the right place for him." Seb isn't angry, he hasn't even raised his voice, but his eyes are icy.

"Where should we take him?" I say, knowing the answer.

"Home."

I turn away, and stare out of the window. The sky fills with starlings, throwing shapes against the blue, and then they're gone. We fall into an uneasy silence. He's right. Of course Scottie belongs in the Field.

"When this is all over, I'll take him back," I say, finally. Seb doesn't respond.

*   *   *

There is no breeze, even though all four windows have been cranked open. I'm melting. I yearn for the misty Island drizzle, the wet winds. The road changes from rocky track to potholed tarmac and back again, potholes, craters, dirt. We descend into a narrow valley, sloping green hills either side of the track. A moment in the shade. Huge signposts mark the road, but whatever was written on them has long faded as black smudges point the way to nowhere.

The hills flatten out as we approach a series of low buildings, some made of stone, some of wood. Trees curl around their brickwork, broad leaves for curtains. Crows shriek into the sky as we sail past. Further on, deep woodland; a deer and her fawn race through the trees, chased by orange butterflies.

"Can we stop soon?" I gasp. "I need to get out of this car, just for a few minutes."

"No." Zan doesn't take her eyes off the road. Silence once more.

We leave the woodland and the sun disappears for a moment behind a single grey cloud, throwing the landscape into shadow.

By the time we've wound our way onto the coast road it's raining; a refreshing breeze blows in off the sea. On one side the water stretches out below us, the shore lined with the rotting skeletons of gigantic boats slumped on their sides. Seagulls scream. On the other side, ancient, junked cars have been shoved into the foothills—a jumble of metal and gorse. Awake now, Scottie stares sullenly out of the window. Giving his hand a squeeze, I wonder if he's missing Noah, but of course he's not. He wants his mum and dad. I don't have any words for him right now. I want mine too.

The sky is a solid grey when we finally stop at the Bridge. We stretch and yawn into the cool wind, a relief from the pounding sun. The twins throw cartwheels in the grass. Noah tries to keep up with their spinning bodies, but can't. Gregor hands round water and dry, salty biscuits.

We stand before the towering stone arch leading to a bridge that's so long it disappears into the mist ahead. The red paint has worn off in huge patches revealing the rusty steel beneath. Sections of the overhead supports have also fallen away. It is magnificent and it looks like it's dying. Its size alone takes my breath away. There is nothing to compare it to. The sea beneath its struts is a mass of churning greys. The faces of the Giften show excitement, anticipation and fear. I don't know what I feel. This Bridge is more than a road to them, it's the doorway between the Island and the City. The City, where the Sanctuary and the Circle will finally meet in underground rooms to plan their attack.

Where I'll see Dev again.

"The Bridge wasn't built for cars," Zan explains. "But for *trains*. MAGs have been useful for once, though."

Beyond the arch are two sets of narrow steel tracks. The space between one set has been filled with small stones, the width of two solars. Two other bridges cross the sea to our right, the middle of each having plunged into the water long ago.

"Do what you need to do," says Zan scanning the horizon. "And then we're off."

Noah climbs onto the roof of a solar, peering through binos along the length of the Bridge.

"Looks clear," he tells us.

"Remember, we go in hard if we meet resistance." And then Zan turns to me and Stace and Seb. "Not you though. You stay out of it."

This is real, I think, a thrill of fear racing down my arms into my hands. Stace is staring at Zan in awe, even though she's just been told to *stay out of it*. This can't be what she imagined life outside the Field would look like. Maybe it's better, more exciting. Even the danger hasn't fazed her, yet.

Back in the solar, Seb sits up front with Zan and we've lost Scottie to Noah's car.

The solars bump along so slowly on the pebbly surface it would be quicker to walk. In the sky, thick grey clouds are displaced by darker grey clouds. The bright sun and the heat are distant memories. Spits of rain splatter the windscreen. A tingle sparks up my spine: the impossible heat of the morning and now the rain, it means only one thing: storm.

On the other set of tracks, a three-carriage train looms into view, silent and stationary. I try to picture the people who once crossed over the water in this vast machine. What did they talk about? The drizzle has suddenly picked up, driving through the smashed-out windows like reverse tears pouring into empty eye sockets.

Our breath starts to fog up the windscreen and Zan wipes it with her sleeve.

She clamps down hard on the brake.

Zan leans out of her window, lifting her binos. When she pulls back inside her T-shirt and hair are drenched.

"Solars," she says. "Definitely two. Hard to see."

The hammering of rain on the solar becomes a warning.

"Shall we go back?" I say, and instantly regret my words. This is the Sanctuary. They don't run away.

A shadow crosses my window. Gregor, huge and wet, leaning into the car.

"What do you think?" he asks. Rain glistens in his black beard.

Zan shakes her head slowly. "Let's keep moving."

Only one windscreen wiper works, and it wouldn't matter if it didn't, it's impossible to see more than a few feet ahead. Seb is bolt upright in his seat. We could be moving towards our deaths. Or the other cars might just be people on a Supply Run. When we're three quarters of the way along the Bridge, the downpour eases for a split second and we see, very clearly, two black solars creeping towards us side by side. There's no way to get past them.

"They're waving at us to stop," Zan says quietly, and then, "*I* talk."

Through the pulsing rain we watch the black cars approach. My nails sink into my palms once more. They stop and three MAGs step out. Each of them is holding a gun.

"Everybody out of your solars!"

19

Twenty-five years ago I joined a team of explorers and scientists, desperate to find out what became of your land. Expecting to find a country devoid of human life, we encountered the communities instead; pockets of survivors living off fertile earth. Your buildings fallen into ruin or swallowed by the floods, you started from scratch, making shelters from whatever materials still existed. You handed down any knowledge you had of life before the Darkening to the generations that came after. You lived or died by the weather.

SAIGE, THE CITY

leven of us stand in a long line against the rusty railings of the Bridge. The rain is fierce and the sky rumbles overhead as the sea boils below. I shelter Scottie inside my waterproof, as much from the MAGs as from the downpour. His small body shakes. The faces of Annis, Alia, Gregor, Zan, Noah and the other Giften are blank. They show neither fury nor fear. I don't know what mine is doing. I'm trying to stay in the moment. Here on the Bridge. I try not to see the bodies of my friends disappearing beneath the waves, as we're thrown over the side. One by one.

Three MAGs stand before us; guns hang from their hands, dripping water. Thick black trousers cling to their legs like wrinkled skin. The steady rain blurs their edges.

Dressed identically, the MAGs could be triplets, but fear is making me blind. The one speaking wears a grey woollen hat pulled down so low on his forehead it almost covers his eyes. One of them has short, tight, blond curls and the third has only one eye.

"Tell me the name of your community again."

"Foxbarks," says Zan. "Way up north."

"Never heard of it," says the MAG, turning to the other MAGs.

"Think I have. Coastal community. Is that right?" Curly Hair asks and Zan nods.

"We're heading to the City. Hoping to settle." Her voice is loud above the rain. Confident. She has told him our story. Our community has failed, we're travelling to the City in the hope of food and shelter. But they want to hear it again and again.

"What is a little strange," Grey Hat says, "is that you all look way too healthy for a starving community." He snorts.

The rain doesn't seem to bother them. They're *enjoying* this, I think.

"What's wrong with the kid?" The one-eyed MAG points with his gun at the bump of Scottie still hidden inside my coat. I feel Scottie flinch and then become very still. I draw him closer.

Noah tenses beside me. Grey Hat sees it too.

"He's... He's just cold," I stammer.

But the MAG is looking at Noah. "And you, tough guy? Problem?"

"No problem," says Noah slowly, showing the MAG his palms. "He's just a kid, he's cold and a bit scared. Can you blame him?"

Zan is staring at Noah.

Thunder cracks overhead. A streak of lightning rips through the clouds; everyone ducks as it strikes the cables overhead. I imagine the Bridge cracking in two, my body falling into the sea.

"Let's see you, kid." Grey Hat gestures once more at Scottie.

I slowly pull back my jacket and the boy peers up into the MAG's wet face. His lips are moving, whispering the same words over and over. *Don't kill us, don't kill us.*

"Hey, it's OK, Scottie." Noah steps out of the line and sinks to his haunches, taking Scottie's hands in his. "We'll be on our way soon. Hey, look at *me*, OK, not him."

But Scottie is transfixed by the man in black.

"Back in line!" Grey Hat snaps.

Noah stands up slowly and turns around. "He's just a kid. A scared kid."

"Back in line!" Rain soaks the woollen hat. The MAG's arms are covered in red goosebumps.

"Noah!" Zan's voice cuts the pounding rain, the thrashing waters below, but he doesn't seem to hear her.

Very slowly I hook my fingers into the waistband of his trousers and gently tug. Grey Hat sinks to his haunches just as Noah had done, his face level with Scottie's. The MAGs draw closer, but they're not scared of a bunch of nobodies on the road. They've even holstered their guns.

"What are you saying, kid?" Grey Hat's voice is softer now, like he really wants to know.

In response, and before I can stop him, Scottie shoves the MAG, who loses his balance, tumbling onto his backside. Everyone freezes. I glance at Zan; her expression is unreadable. I lift Scottie onto my hip and he buries his face in my neck and begins to sob.

"He's not well," I say. "He has a fever, he—"

"Stop talking!" Grey Hat yells, getting to his feet. "Say you're sorry." He pokes Scottie in the ribs but the boy won't show his face.

"Come on, Jed," One Eye says. "Let's get going. I'm freezing out here. They're not worth it."

Another streak of lightning flashes across the sky and the rain intensifies, drumming out its warnings. Every inch of me is wet and Scottie is heavy. I look into the faces of the Giften, just as blank as Zan's.

"That kid attacked me. He needs to say sorry," the MAG is saying. His lips curl into a cruel smile.

It's his smile that does it, telling me that a young boy's fear means nothing to him, to them. My heart rate slows as an intense heat starts to build in my hands; it travels up into my arms and chest. The MAG pulls off his hat and squeezes out rainwater. He swipes it at Scottie's back and instinctively I reach out and catch his wrist as he goes to swipe again.

The MAG's flesh is cold, firm and wet. His people killed this boy's community, his parents; they did it just because they could. And they're not done. The slow pulse of my heart vibrates into my fingers.

"Don't touch me!" The MAG is furious. "You... you..." He tries to yank his arm away, but I hold on for a few seconds longer and then I let go, as repulsed by him as he is by me. Before he can say another mean word he humphs out a small gasp and hits the ground. A livid red patch has appeared around his wrist. My mouth opens and closes.

The other two MAGs stare at Grey Hat, transfixed. But then Zan is moving. Noah and the twins and Gregor are moving. Their feet leave the ground as they leap.

Zan rips the gun out of Curly Hair's holster before he can reach it, whipping the hilt across his face. He falls onto his knees, his nose broken and bleeding. Scottie is screaming.

One Eye was faster, he's firing blindly as Noah and Gregor charge him. I duck; a bullet misses my head by inches. I smell burning hair for an instant and then it's gone. Scottie stops screaming. He's shivering, terrified.

Noah and Gregor and One Eye go down, punching, grappling. The gun flies out of the MAG's hand. The men slide over the wet ground as they strike and pummel. The rain comes down. The MAG knows he's fighting for his life, he knows if he loses this, he loses everything. It's horrible to watch, but I can't look away. Neither can Stace or Seb. Noah is on top of One Eye, straddling his chest, his hands around his neck.

Zan kicks Curly Hair in the stomach, he doubles over and she's turning, moving towards Noah and the one-eyed MAG. She presses a hand to his face as he tries to squirm away from her. But it's too late; she's burned him. Rainwater fills his empty eye-socket and overflows.

Curly Hair is still on his knees, one hand on his stomach and the other trying to staunch the blood flowing from his nose. The rain is slowing. I tear my eyes away to look up into the sky. It's clearing; seagulls wheel overhead, screaming into the wind.

I lower Scottie to the ground. "It's over, OK? You're safe."

We gather around the only conscious MAG.

"Who… who are you?" he says, his voice barely audible.

"You know who we are," Zan says.

"I-I—"

"Tell me who we are!"

He opens his mouth but nothing comes out.

"Say it."

"The… the Sanctuary," he whispers. When she nods, Curly Hair forgets about his nose and his stomach and covers his face, sobbing. Tears and blood pour through his fingers.

"You should have killed us when you had the chance," says Alia.

"Now we get to kill you." Annis steps closer and he rears away, sliding on the wet ground until he's flat on his back. The blood pumps from his nose. "How many of us have you cried for?" She leans over and slaps him hard across the face.

"Please," he begs. "I have a kid too." He looks at Scottie. "A daughter."

"Why do you think we care?" says Zan. "You've taken our children and killed our parents." She flexes her fingers, as if she's itching to burn him.

I burned a MAG for the first time. To save Scottie.

"We've heard the stories," Zan is saying. "The experiments. Trying to steal our gift for yourselves. You can't do it, can you?" When the MAG shuts his eyes, Zan roars, "Can you?"

The wind is dropping too, as if the weather is waiting for his answer.

But the MAG is still crying. "She hasn't done it yet," he says between sobs. "But why is it so bad? Who doesn't want to be Giften, to save the land, and… and feed people?"

The tension is back in my fingers. I let go of Scottie's hand fast and I'm moving past the others. The MAG tries to shuffle away as I approach, but Zan nudges him with her boot and he stops moving.

"Feed people? You?" I rage. "*You* take our food. *You* take our Giften. They *never* come back and we *starve!*"

The blood pounds in my head. Everyone else has vanished. It's just me and this... this MAG on a broken-down bridge over a raging sea.

"You're not heroes," I spit. "You didn't have to become a MAG. None of you did. You made a gregious choice!" I want to *burn* this MAG too. I want revenge for Scottie, for Joshie.

"My dad was a Rover," he says desperately. "You don't know what it was like for him, for any of us. Growing up on the *outside*. We were shunned by every single community. We didn't choose that either. And... and we're not all the same," he looks at me, "I'm not the same as him or him." He points to the other MAGs and shivers. "Give me a chance. I'll take the uniform off right now. I'll disappear... I'll—"

"Stop talking!" shouts Annis. She turns to Zan. "Let's do this and get on the road."

Zan makes a slicing motion across her throat, nodding at Noah and Gregor. The MAG starts to scrabble away as the men take hold of him. I call Scottie and head towards our solar. Once the little boy is inside, I look back to see Gregor and Noah drop the screaming, struggling curly-haired MAG over the side of the Bridge.

This is what revenge looks like, and it makes me feel sick.

"Ruthie!" Noah is running towards me. Behind him Annis and Alia have One Eye. They count to three and tip him over too. I can't meet Noah's eyes, so I stare at his boots.

"They're *MAGs*," he says, breathlessly, his fingers reaching for my cheek. "This is the only way they can be taught. I *know* what it looks like." Behind him, in the misty rain, Zan and Gregor launch the last of the MAGs over the side. "But this is who we are." His hand falls away from my face. He clenches and unclenches his fists; I can almost hear the vibration in his fingers. "We couldn't let them go."

"They weren't dead though, were they?" Seb is speaking my thoughts as he appears beside Noah. His hair is a wet sheet plastered to his head, his eyes two dark holes.

"Seb, let's not do this now." I reach for him but he jumps at my touch, as if he's scared I'll burn *him* too.

"Are you really *OK* with all of this, Ruthie? Because a few days ago you were just a girl in the Field."

Noah opens his mouth to speak, but I hold up a hand.

"I don't know what I am," I say.

The doors of the MAGs' black solars are wide open; the Giften reach inside, taking guns, food, water. Stace heaves as she empties her stomach over the railings. She turns around, catches my eye and wipes her mouth.

"Stace," I call.

She nods and starts to head over, but Seb is still glaring at me.

"Right now, we just need to keep moving," I say, stepping into the car.

"I asked you a question, though. Ruthie, are you *OK* with how these people do things?" He grabs my arm and pulls me around to face him.

"Hey, cut it out," Noah says. He pushes Seb, hard.

"You can fight me, Noah. You could probably kill me." Seb holds his position. His voice is tight, like he's trying not to cry. "But you can't blame me for looking out for *her*. You're killers. Just like them."

Stace takes his arm. "*They're* the monsters, Seb," she says. Her eyes are wild.

"Who, Stace? The MAGs or the Sanctuary?" he says tightly, not taking his eyes off Noah.

*   *   *

When we're on the road again I think about the MAG and his daughter. What did he tell her about his job? He probably lied to her every day. And Dad—hadn't he lied to me too? All those Supply Runs. They couldn't be more different, these men who shield their daughters from the truth, but they share an absolute certainty that the truth is dangerous.

I don't want to be sheltered any longer; I want to see the world exactly as it is. My hands aren't tingling or vibrating or hot.

Are you OK with this? Seb had asked me. No one is more shocked than me to find out that I am.

20

Some of the soil samples we collected contained extraordinary levels of nitrogen, phosphorus and potassium. It was revelatory. But it was the discovery of the Giften that changed everything—it was like finding out magic was real. If the 'gift' was a virus— my field is epidemiology—what other diseases might lie dormant in the fertile earth of the North? I needed to study the Giften from the comfort of my labs in the South, and with promises of adventure many came back with me, willingly enough.

SAIGE, THE CITY

I feel the City drawing closer. There's a change in the air, a new smell, a *heaviness*. The sky is clear and the heat more a blanket than an oven by late afternoon; there's even a small breeze.

We join a wide tarmac road, free of potholes. Rusty cars are stacked in neat columns of three or four in the long grass, either side of the track.

"They're clearing the land, all part of the grand plan to expand the City," says Zan. "They'll be dumping this lot up country soon enough."

The cars fall away and we're driving through woodland again. The sun flashes through the leaves, a hopeful signal that all will be well. The silhouette of a different skyline appears in the far distance. Not the soft outline of trees or mountains but the straight edges of brick buildings, hazy in the low light of the afternoon. The air is charged with a different smell, a dusty, metallic stink.

Long-faded signs line the road. Leaving the woodland we pass long-abandoned buildings, reduced to their stone foundations, ravaged by wild vegetation; silent spaces with black gaping holes for windows. A tall burned-out tree stands alone in the field behind the ruins. Crows squat on every branch.

Noah, in the back of the solar, focuses his binos on the road behind.

"What?" Stace asks.

Noah has slid open his window, he's half in, half out of the car, signalling to the other cars to speed up.

"Solars," he says. "Couple of miles back."

Leaning out of my own window I squint to see three tiny black smudges on a distant hill.

Zan sighs. "We're almost at the shelter now in any case." The battery is low, and the light is fading. "We don't need another MAG face-off right now."

"MAGs?" Scottie is on his knees on the back seat; his face pressed against the rear window. He turns around to look at Zan.

"Don't worry," she says, forcing a smile. "We have a hidey hole."

Scottie relaxes, but he's the only one.

Zan pulls off the road onto a narrow gorse-lined dirt track, the other two solars in the convoy directly behind us. She pulls up and takes a long knife from her belt.

"Need to hide our tracks," she says. "You guys have whittling knives?" she asks.

For the next few minutes, all of us bend to the task of ripping and tearing at the gorse and bramble and with scratched and bleeding hands we drag the bushes onto the mouth of the path.

Then we're bumping along a dirt road. More junked cars and rubbled shelters loom ahead of us, sunlight glancing off metal and broken glass. Zan guides the solars through a wide doorway into the only building still standing; a large low-ceilinged space. Easily four times the size of the Shed, the property squats in the centre of the rusty remains of ancient machines, maybe even farming machines, I think, staring at the corroded steel teeth of a gigantic contraption poised at the entrance.

This building has somehow escaped the creeping foliage that wraps itself around every structure I have seen since I left the Field. Only thin lines of ivy stream up the concrete slab walls. The ceiling is made of thick frosted glass or plastic.

The twins aren't spinning cartwheels, and no one even speaks as we head back outside. The Giften stand ready, aiming bows and guns up the track. Stace is holding my hand, her cold fingers squeeze mine painfully. Seb reaches an arm across our shoulders. It seems that in the face of danger we're united. And I'm glad. I feel him tense, draw us closer as the hum of solars erupts into the air. And then it's fading. They glide past.

"OK, then," says Zan, exhaling slowly. She wipes sweat from her forehead.

"So that's it? They're gone?" I say, confused. "But they must have seen us."

Everyone looks pale despite the golden light of the setting sun.

Gregor forces a smile. "Maybe," he says. "Probably. But maybe they had someone else to chase. They've gone in any case. And we've nowhere else to hide. So let's take it as a win." He points at Noah. "You and the twins, take the solars round to the back of the building. Catch the last of the sun." Heading back inside the building, he flicks on a storm torch. "Come on," he calls. "Time to eat."

As we pick at the last of the dried meat and bread, the light fades. Overhead, the sun becomes a small orange ball in the sky.

"We'll be leaving in a few hours, when it's dark. So get some sleep now." Zan yawns and stretches.

I stare at my hands. The heat is back. But it's not the Burn. It's the desire for a different kind of release. The tips of my fingers look swollen. I think that if I pricked them long jets of bright red blood would spurt out. I join the rest of the Giften outside to make mud. The moment my fingers scoop up the earth, the tension eases and I put the black solars out of my mind.

I hand out mats from the car boot of one solar, keeping back four for me and my friends. But when I go back inside Seb isn't there.

"He's not saying much," says Stace, laying out a mat for Scottie and then for herself. "I'd let him be for a bit."

*   *   *

I can't sleep, my fingers are still tingling. I move slowly and silently through the room, tiptoeing past the dreaming bodies. I would read Logan's records if there was enough light, but what I really need is to make more mud.

"Ruthie?" Noah's face looms out of the dark as I settle on my haunches, my fingers already deep in the earth, the familiar warmth flooding through me. I feel like I've been caught doing something I shouldn't.

"I'm just—I was…" I mumble, pulling my hands free.

"Couldn't sleep?" He shows me his own muddy hands and then offers me a leather pouch of water to rinse off the dirt. He points to the silver sliver in the sky. It glows a cold white in the clear black. "No MAGs up there," he says, taking back the pouch and dropping it by his feet.

In this small scrub of earth, surrounded by rusty machines, a giant concrete wall at our backs, for just a minute there's pure silence; so quiet I imagine I can hear the passage of the moon.

"And meeting the Circle, that's a whole other thing. Don't get your hopes up. Plenty like Eshe in the Sanctuary."

The nails of scurrying wildlife skitter on the metal junk as Noah talks.

"How old were you when you joined the Sanctuary?" I don't want to think about Eshe, or the Circle, for just a few minutes.

Noah laughs, his shoulder bumping mine as he squats down beside me. "Taking my history?"

We lock eyes. And before I know what I'm doing I'm running a finger over the dimple in his cheek. He catches my wrist as I pull away fast, appalled, praying it's too dark for him to see my red face. He holds my fingers against his cheek. He has a line of freckles on his nose and the tops of his cheeks. Looking into those grey eyes in the dim light, my heart starts to slam.

"Ruthie?" he says softly, still holding on to my hand. He leans forward until our faces are inches apart.

"What?" I whisper, but he doesn't answer.

Maybe it's because I can't stop thinking about Dad, can't help missing Mum, or I'm scared of the *Burn*, the City, a million things—but right now, more than anything else, I don't want to feel alone. So I close the gap between our faces and kiss his smiling mouth.

Noah lets go of my hand and laces his fingers through my hair, drawing me closer still. I think of his teasing, of the blue bracelet laid in my palm, his shoulder pressing into mine just now—was it all leading to this moment? And then I don't think about anything at all.

"Ruthie, what are you doing?"

My eyes snap open and I pull away from Noah to see Seb, his white hair a beacon in the moonlight. I stand up fast, but Noah doesn't move.

"I... I..." But there are no words for this, it's obvious.

Seb turns away from me to face the track leading to the road. He's holding a wind-up torch.

"Doesn't matter," he says, his voice no more than a whisper. And then he starts up the track towards the road.

"Where are you going?" I ask. "Seb?"

But he doesn't answer.

"Don't get lost," calls Noah, rising to his feet.

Seb stops but doesn't turn around. "I won't," he says and sets off again.

Noah and I stand in silence, watching him disappear up the track and into the darkness beyond. I feel guilty, a little ashamed. Seb was loyal to his word and I knew how he felt about me.

"Idiot," Noah says. "Bloody kid. For the love of—"

A screech of tyres peals through the night air; loud voices erupt from the road. Noah and I freeze.

"IN THE CAR!" A booming voice from the road; an order. A car door slams, then another.

"MAGs!" I whisper frantically. "They're here!"

Noah reaches for his bow, but it's not there. He grabs my arm, his face is suddenly very pale. "Go back inside, wake Zan and the others," he whispers, and then he's crouching low and running towards the road.

By the time everyone is armed and racing down the track, Seb is gone. The air is still and the road empty.

"It was a black solar," sighs Noah. "MAGs got him." He looks at me and Stace. "I'm sorry."

Stace is crying into her hands, but I feel numb.

A scrape of rubber on the road is the only sign anyone was here at all.

"Get your stuff together," shouts Zan as we head back to the shelter. "We need to get out of here fast. Soon enough he'll tell them about us, torture it out of him most likely. We're lucky they didn't come looking." She exchanges a look with Gregor, he shakes his head slowly.

"They just grabbed a lone boy? Why?"

No one answers, but I think I can guess. By now, maybe the MAGs have found out Dad wasn't travelling alone. Maybe they're looking for a boy with shockingly white hair. But what about the two girls and the other boy? Why didn't they come for us?

That isn't all I'm not saying: if he hadn't seen me with Noah, maybe Seb wouldn't have wandered off and got himself ambushed.

21

My experiments took their toll on the Giften, so I sent for more as and when I needed them. It sounds brutal to you, doesn't it—killing people for science? But the Giften might very well represent another stage in our evolution and to understand it, I had to take them apart, as you would a machine.

SAIGE, THE CITY

he solars split up as we enter the City; three cars heading in the same direction is a risk. Even in darkness.

With each turn of the wheel something grinds inside my chest. If I had taken just five minutes to talk to Seb he might be with us in the car right now.

My eyes are gritty from lack of sleep and my head pounds.

"We'll find him in the City," Stace says, more to herself than to me. "Just like we'll find Dan."

"I don't know your friend," says Zan. "But I know MAGs. If he's weak they'll get the whole thing out of him."

"He's not weak!" Stace says. "It's a mistake. Maybe they thought he was someone else. What was he doing on the road anyway?" She turns to me. "Did he say anything to you? You saw him last, didn't you?"

I don't meet her eyes and instead, look out of the window into the night sky. "He said he was going for a walk."

*   *   *

The wheels of the solar crunch over pine cones littering the road into the City. Ancient destruction surrounds us, vast spaces where buildings once stood, now just mountains of rubble. This landscape of demolition transforms into wide streets where crumbling buildings sit still and silent. Shells of homes, yawning spaces where rooms should be. Craters and potholes in the road have been filled with bricks and sand.

But the wilderness still dominates. There are hushed streets where new trees fight for space with older, bigger trees. Solar lamps on long poles in the ground emit a soft yellow light showing where the vegetation has pushed itself into what were once people's bedrooms and kitchens. Wildlife scuttles up and down the walls and rummages in the bushes which swamp the foundations. Rabbits, squirrels, foxes.

We pass roads of squat, narrow houses, rebuilt from salvaged stone, their walls uneven and roofs lined with solar panels. Light beams from between the cracks in wooden shutters. But elsewhere, woodland has grown around the carcasses of ruin.

To stop myself picturing Seb in a dungeon with Dad, I think about the order and beauty of the Field, our neat rows of cropland, our magnificent Woods sheltering us from the outside world; the Clearing where we gather to celebrate. Where do people gather in the City? What do they celebrate? There is something disturbing about the lights behind the shuttered windows too, I picture people hiding in isolation. The smell in the early morning air isn't of baking, but instead the stink of rotting fruit and unwashed clothes. Stace squeezes my fingers as we take it all in.

We drive down a road that has a single house standing amidst the rubble. The faces of three smallies are pressed against a grimy window. They watch us glide past with wide eyes.

We see only one other solar; its driver a lone woman with a long face who doesn't even glance in our direction as she drives slowly past.

"They're all like that in the City," says Zan. "Head down, shuffling along."

"They could live anywhere," says Stace. "Why here?"

But she knows why. We all do. I think back to Logan's oral histories telling stories of the disabled, the old and the abandoned, coming to the City for food and shelter.

The sky is brighter and I sense Zan's impatience to get to the Tombs. Her head is almost on the windscreen as we turn down a narrow road lined with small wooden shelters. Just a single solar lamp in the middle of the street shines a weak light over the cobbles.

The road is a dead end; the thick straight trunks of chestnut trees loom up in the distance. The cobbles become a thin dirt track and we're driving through woodland. I let out a breath, but my relief is short-lived. Out of the woods we find ourselves in open space, where rubble has been cleared away and the foundations for rows of small buildings have been laid. The wheels of the solar kick up clouds of dust.

"We're nearly there." Zan gives a tight smile.

We drive through the construction site, towards the silhouette of stone remains, where whole buildings have fallen on their sides, toppled by events I cannot imagine. Debris skitters onto the roof of the solar as we rumble past.

At last Zan parks outside the remains of a low black brick building in a wilderness of grass long enough to hide in. Its foundations cast a wide circle of empty space overflowing with gorse and brambles and long grass.

"They haven't demolished this part of the City yet," explains Zan. "But they will. And soon, probably. This might be our last meeting at the Tombs."

"Maybe we won't need the Tombs or any safe houses," says Noah. "If we do this thing."

Zan fixes him with a steady gaze. "We're doing this *thing* one step at a time. Let's see who turns up first," she says.

"They'll all be there, Zan. Everyone. They believe in *you*."

"This is about more than my charm as a leader." Zan's eyes flash.

She leads us towards a heavy wooden door, as black as the brickwork. Beside it are the gaping holes where two other doors once stood. She thumps three times. The door opens into darkness and a young woman steps out of the gloom.

"Thank God you're here," she says breathlessly, stepping aside. "There's trouble."

Zan flicks on her torch and we follow her down wide stone steps. It's all long shadows and dark corners; yellow light from wall-mounted fire torches flickers on the damp stone walls. The smell of animal faeces is strong. Through a short tunnel we enter a wide corridor, where low-ceilinged, domed rooms branch off left and right, dark and dank. Zan heads for the room directly ahead; beyond a brick archway. More fire torches illuminate the figures whose angry voices bounce off the dripping walls.

In the middle of the room, surrounded by forty or fifty Giften, Gregor stands between Alia and another woman, his arms spread wide, while the women reach across him to swipe and kick at each other. Everyone is shouting, their bows quivering on their backs.

Is this over before it's even begun?

"We have to find Scottie," I tell Stace, beginning a circuit of the room.

Strangers glance away from the fight to look us up and down, suspicion in their eyes. I find the boy huddled in a corner with his hands over his ears.

"Hey, kid," says Stace, crouching down to hug him. "Let's you and me explore this place." She hoists him onto her hip and leads him out of the main chamber.

"For the gregious love of the land," Zan is saying, her voice low, angry. "This is the Sanctuary; are you Giften or are you animals?" She doesn't wait for an answer, but points at a woman from the advance boat party, one of those tasked with calling the Giften to the Tombs. "Is this everyone?"

"People are still arriving, Zan, don't worry. The word went out as planned to all the City safe houses."

Like everyone else in the room I find myself leaning in to hear Zan's words.

"You're angry; I get it. All you took from my message was, *Zan wants us to join the Circle*." No one moves or speaks. "Do you think I've lost my mind?" Again, silence. "But you *are* here, which means you are more curious than furious. You are willing, at the very least, to listen."

"The *Circle*, Zan?" A man, as big as Gregor, steps forward, his muscly arms crossed over his broad chest. "We came to look you in the eye and ask if you're serious. We—"

"Speak for yourself, Craig!" says another voice. "I came here to *listen*."

"Eshe chose not to listen. You can do the same, Craig," says Alia. She looks ready to fight him too.

"My eyes are right here, Craig. Look deep into them and understand I'm serious." Zan pauses to gather and twist her dreads into a heap, securing them on top of her head with a thin stick she has pulled from her belt. "Graylings, Ottoway. Who's next? They're taking out whole communities while we hang on to our rage for what happened *five years* ago on the Ravelston Road," she says.

Craig puffs out his chest, stands straighter. "The Circle killed our people. They blundered into something they had no idea how to finish and *we* died. Damn right we're angry."

Other voices erupt from the crowd, some shouting him down, others shouting support. I find myself moving through the room, pushing past the Giften until I'm beside Zan. I didn't go to Foundation Island for it all to fall apart now.

My hands sing a familiar vibration. I think of the tall grass outside and wish I'd taken a moment to make mud.

In the flickering light, all I see are angry and confused faces.

"I'm Ruthie. I'm Giften," I say, clenching and unclenching my fists. "I've seen Graylings." The figures shuffle closer. "The little boy who arrived with the twins? That's Scottie. He's the Giften child the MAGs were hunting. They *wiped out* his whole community because they couldn't find him."

Craig sighs and looks at his boots.

Everyone else is watching me.

A hand on my back. Annis. "Go on," she says.

"They beat them before they killed them and then dumped their bodies in a shed; kids, parents, the elders, side by side." I close my eyes at the memory. "And then I met the Circle. I met Ian and Mairie. They're not monsters and they're not crazy. They just want to talk. That's why I'm here, to ask you to let them in. All I want is to live on my land, with my people, eat the food we grow without MAGs stealing it and killing the Giften who raised it." Angry faces relax and sad ones smile. "Scottie is the reason we should fight the MAGs *together*."

A warm hand takes mine. Noah, his eyes glisten in the dancing torchlight.

"Zan, please." Craig is speaking again, but his voice is softer now. "You're asking us to fight alongside people who don't care who dies as long as they win." He gives a long sigh and shakes his head. "But I'll hear them out."

A series of loud thumps on the wooden door echoes through the tunnels. This happens again and again, until the room slowly fills with more Giften: the Sanctuary. I watch Zan with Noah, her mouth to his ear. He gives a comical salute and leaves.

The rumble of voices grows louder, more excited, as Zan circulates; the stuffy room is too warm. I wander the dark passages and domed spaces looking for a pot of earth in which to bury my hands. Finding neither I come back into the main room.

And there is Dev. At last. Soon I will tell him about Seb.

Noah, Ian, Dev and Mairie stand under the stone archway and the room falls silent. Zan approaches and we watch Noah introduce the Circle to his leader. A gasp sweeps the room as Zan holds out her hand. Ian takes it, and leans in, talking into her ear. When she eventually turns to face the room, she's serious, unsmiling.

"I have my doubts, like the rest of you. But we have lost Graylings and we have lost Ottoway. Communities slaughtered for their Giften." She rests a hand over her heart. "This man isn't our enemy. Even those who attacked the MAG convoy on Ravelston Road and killed fifty of our own were not our enemies." A quiet muttering breaks out; Zan raises her voice. "The Circle was careless; so full of bloodlust for the MAGs it blinded them. And *we* suffered, we lost people who we had once saved. It's hard to forgive, impossible to forget." She nods at Ian.

He hasn't taken his eyes off the crowd of two hundred Giften who stand before him. "In three days' time the Circle will attack the Base at midnight," he begins. His blond spiky hair catches the golden light; beside Zan he looks like a boy, but he doesn't sound like one. "This will be the first and last fight, because either the MAGs will die or we will." Ian pauses for a moment to let his words sink in.

I move through the crowd to the front of the room. I need Dev right now, his solid presence. He reaches for my hand and draws me close. His familiar smell. It feels like months.

"I am not here to make excuses for the past. If I was you, I would feel the same." Ian glances at Zan. "Five years ago the Circle was just a group of angry people, attacking MAGs, risking the lives of our own families for revenge. The Circle *hated* the MAGs more than they cared about anything else. After Ravelston Road the group fell apart. Everything changed. Today we have a structure, leaders; we research our missions, we plan and we prepare. Ravelston Road could never happen again." Ian nods at me. "Ruthie's father. He turned us around. He made us fit for the mission ahead. We can't win on bloodlust. And we might not be able to win at all without you."

I take in this information slowly; if Dev's arms weren't around my shoulders I might fall.

Dad wasn't just part of the Circle; he'd been rebuilding them. Ever since Ravelston Road.

"Your carelessness cost lives." Craig steps out of the crowd and moves towards Ian. The two men are face to face. Craig jabs a finger into Ian's chest. Ian doesn't react, doesn't move an inch.

Gregor takes a step too, but Zan shakes her head.

"We need to see these plans, this research," Craig says.

Ian smiles. "You will."

"Go and fetch your people, Ian, these *leaders* and let's start," Zan says.

I sense something has changed for the Giften. The monsters have been unmasked, and they look just like us.

22

The short-sightedness of my peers was astounding. I was thwarted by the ethical concerns of those too stupid to understand my ambition. Yes, Giften died, but this was research, this was science. They wanted to lock me up, take my daughter away from me. But, as you know, that never happened. I fled to the North with Lily. With help from the sympathetic amongst the scientific community, I armed your Rovers, rebuilt the Base and my work continued. I would pass on the Gift to anyone who wanted it. I would change the fortunes of the entire world.

SAIGE, THE CITY

n hour ago two dozen Circle members came through the arched entrance into the cramped spaces of the Tombs. What would three hundred of them look like? A warrior army of men and women, with bows on their backs, a scoop of arrows on their hips, the bulge of weapons under their patchwork shirts. Not so different to the Sanctuary.

In small teams, spread out in the main room and in the domed chambers, Sanctuary and Circle bend their heads to the job of war. In these hot spaces, bathed in yellow light from flaming torches, I watch the shoulders of old enemies brush as maps are produced.

"Right now," Mairie explains to my group, "the MAGs are in the City, planning their own missions to collect the autumn Offerings. So, we go in now or we go in next year."

The combined forces of Sanctuary and Circle are roughly equivalent to the number of MAGs at the Base, around six hundred souls. And the plan? A surprise attack in the early hours of the morning to disable or wipe out the Base—and Saige Corentin. These simple sentences can be spoken in a moment, but how long to enact them? To fight, draw blood and kill? I have no idea. I'm not a fighter.

But first, a reconnaissance mission to the City. Tomorrow, just a couple of hours before dawn, we will all head into the City in small groups, to learn the route and scout for trouble before we launch our attack the following day.

Even though Stace and I won't join the battle, we still have to be able to find our way back to the Tombs if it all goes wrong. Stace and I have another job. And then, when we're done, we will hide in the shadows of thick bushes and tall trees around the Base, until the fighting is over and I can go inside and rescue Dad.

And Seb. And maybe even Joshie.

"Seb's no use to them," Dev said when we told him about the ambush. "He's not a fighter and he's not Giften. They've probably let him go already. If not, we'll find him." Dev has changed or maybe I just never noticed before. Unlike me, he's not scared of anything.

*   *   *

It had been a short restless night in the Tombs, the room hot and thick with the smell of damp stone walls and rodent droppings. And now, in the fresh pre-dawn air, exhausted and more than a little scared, surrounded by *warriors*, I am about to prowl the City streets looking for trouble. Their breath fogs the air as the Giften wish each other luck and set off towards the MAG house.

Before the Darkening, the land around the MAG HQ was home to abundant gardens of plants and trees, but now it's a wilderness, patrolled by MAGs. In the middle of this wild tangle of undergrowth looms the Base; a vast hive of dormitories and prison cells and rooms where Giften are experimented upon. And that's where we're heading.

"When will I come back, Ruthie?" Scottie's eyes are wet, his cheeks flushed pink by a crisp wind.

"Soon," I say, stroking his hair. I feel a pang for Ant and a fierce need to protect Scottie as I would my baby brother. "We'll be together before you know it." I try to sound confident. But it's obvious from the look in Scottie's eyes, wide and scared, that I don't.

Taking Alia's hand, the boy looks back once more before he's led away to a safe house in the City.

I watch Dev, pulling his hood over his head, checking the weapon in his belt, and then setting off through the grassland with Ian and Mairie and Craig.

"I guess we're on our own then," says Stace, staring after him.

But Dev is turning around, jogging back towards us, drawing us both into a hug. "Might see you outside the Base. But back here later, right?" He lets go. "Stay close to Noah and no heroics."

"Do you mean him or us?" I ask, grinning. And then my smile falls away. This isn't a stomp through the Woods on a sunny day. This isn't the time for jokes.

Just a few hours ago we were settling down to grab a little sleep before our dawn raid. Those hours, I realize now, were a kind of passage between my old life, where I mostly watched other people make speeches, form plans and give orders, and this place, my new reality, where I follow those orders, and try to make a difference. I breathe in the morning air but it does little to make any of this feel real.

*   *   *

In old clothes of deep green and black, hundreds of us begin to creep towards the City streets. Within minutes Stace, Noah and I are alone; everyone has scattered into the dark shadows beneath an overcast sky.

Noah secures a bow to his back, slides a gun into the belt of his trousers, while Stace and I pick up a couple of straw baskets, and follow him.

In silence we cross the construction site and enter the woodland. The air is cool, but not cold. Branches crack under our boots and small animals scatter through the treetops, otherwise it's quiet in the City. I smell the sour, sweet aroma of rotting fruit and animal shit. This will be OK, I tell myself. We'll head to the Base, and then turn around and retrace our footsteps. I will be back in the safety of the Tombs within the hour.

From woodland we emerge onto the cobbled street of the wooden shacks. The single solar lamp in the middle of the road casts an eerie light on the silent shelters.

"You really showed him, didn't you?" A voice cracks the silence and my feet and heart stop, as two shadowy figures round the corner. None of this is OK.

"Keep walking," hisses Noah.

The MAGs move slowly, their pale faces lit up by the glow of the lamp, but their black clothes have blended into the night. They don't see us at first because they're caught up in some sort of argument. About potato wine.

"We give them the gregious potatoes, don't we? Seems right they hand back the liquor they scrounge from it," says one.

"All I'm saying is you didn't have to punch the fella. We coulda just taken the booze and be done with it," the other replies.

"His face was asking for a punch." The men start laughing, but they stop the second they see us.

Our baskets are loaded with windfall, our only excuse for being out this early; picking the best of the fruit before the City wakes up.

They nudge each other. I stare at them with unseeing eyes. Can Noah fight both of them on his own?

"Morning." This MAG has the splash of a purple birthmark creeping up his neck. His belly bulges beneath his shirt. He sways, bumping into the other MAG, who is barely my height, and with an even greater paunch. He has a long thin moustache above his lip, which extends to the centre of each cheek. It looks drawn on.

"Watch it!" says Moustache. "Learn to hold your drink, man." And now I see the heavy glass bottle in Birthmark's hand, half full of sludgy, brown liquid. He lifts it to his mouth, takes a long drink and offers the bottle to Stace.

She shakes her head, staring into her basket. Her knuckles are tight and white around the handle.

"I'll take some," says Noah, smiling wide. "Potato is it?" He holds out a hand but Birthmark ignores him, his attention on Stace.

A sharp wind blows up the dark street and a cloud shifts across the face of the setting moon.

"Go on, take a drink with me, girly," Birthmark sneers, thrusting the bottle into her chest.

Noah takes a step, and so does the other MAG.

"Back off, kid. We're just talking to the pretty girl." Moustache shoves a hand into Noah's chest, pushing him away. Stace and I take a step back. "She your sister?"

"She is," he says.

"That one isn't." The MAG points at me. "She your girlfriend?"

"She is," Noah repeats.

"So," Moustache steps up to Stace, "she can come with us, back for a drink or two, and you can go on your way with your *girlfriend*." Both the MAGs laugh.

My legs feel like they might buckle at any moment, my head feels light. I should be used to this fear by now. They're mean drunks, and Noah hasn't taken his eyes off the MAG who can't take his eyes off Stace.

"After a fight, lad?" Moustache puffs out his chest, he's a full head shorter than Noah.

"We just want to be on our way. That's all." Noah holds up his hands, palms out, and smiles again, but it's a tight, forced grin that doesn't fool anyone. "Windfall," he points at our baskets.

Owls hoot at each other from the treetops. The MAGs raise their faces to the sky, ignoring Noah.

"Mating calls. You hear that?" They're both laughing, leering at Stace.

My legs don't feel weak any more, my heart beats a steady pace. I don't like the way they're looking at my friend. My hands start to tingle and something pops inside my chest. These men aren't like the ones who come into the Field. They are soft where they should have muscle; their stomachs strain against the loose-fitting black shirts that hang over their trousers.

Noah's hand slips to the back of his waistband. Then, we're all turning at the sound of a door creaking open. An old man, bent double, shuffles out of his shack. He freezes when he sees the MAGs. He opens his mouth to speak, but Noah doesn't wait to hear what he's got to say. He's raising his gun, his finger on the trigger.

"No!" I scream. How long before more MAGs stream out of the darkness, alerted by gunfire?

Noah shoots me a look, a question in his eyes. But I should have kept my mouth shut. At the same moment, Birthmark swings the bottle of brown liquid into the side of Noah's head. The thin glass bottle smashes, splashing liquor and shards of glass onto our legs. A sour smell fills the air as Noah collapses.

The old man recovers first, stepping backwards into his house and shutting the door. Stace and I don't move. But Birthmark is swaying. He grabs at Stace to steady himself.

"Don't touch me!" she screams, rearing away. Her voice is a high peal, tearing through the night air.

"Run!" I shout, dropping my basket. I dodge the MAGs and pound the cobbles back towards the woodland. Skidding to a halt just inside the trees, to find that I'm alone. A bitter taste fills my mouth as I turn around and stare into the street.

The MAGs have Stace, but she's fighting back, kicking,

scratching, screaming. Our apples litter the ground and the MAGs trip and slide as she writhes and wriggles out of their clutches. Noah isn't moving. A cold fear starts at my feet and swims up my spine.

Pictures flash through my mind: a *burned* apple, a patch of blistered red skin on the arm of a MAG, Zan's ashy petals. Fear has blinded me to my gift. I stare at my hands; these are my guns, my arrows, my fists. I have lost Dad and Seb. I can't lose Stace.

Keeping close to the shacks, away from the solar lamp, I race back up the road. The old man is watching from his window as Stace drags her nails down Birthmark's cheek; dark blood pours from the scratches onto the purple skin on his neck. Every time they grab her, she twists free. We're lucky they're so drunk.

Their backs are to me as I lunge from the shadows. He doesn't even see me coming. I press my fear, anger and hatred to the bloody scratches on Birthmark's cheeks. Moustache lets go of Stace, swaying as he turns to me, as his friend sinks to the ground. He starts to back away, reaching for his gun.

"You're… you're one of them," he whispers, no longer drunk, no longer so brave. He raises his weapon, but the old man's door creaks open once more. The MAG risks a glance but now he pays the price for hesitating, as an arrow flies past my ear into his chest.

Stace and I jerk round to see Noah, bow in hand, blood on his face, his mouth a thin, grim line.

The MAG's gun clatters to the ground as his hands close around the shaft of the arrow. He falls very slowly, whispering, "*Help me.*"

The old man walks slowly out of his gate and up to the sleeping body of the MAG I just burned. He's holding a stick, sharpened to a point, which he raises with trembling arms and plunges into Birthmark's chest. Stace gasps, pulling me away, but we needn't be scared of the man, the hatred in his eyes is not for us, but for our common enemy.

"Drag them inside," he whispers, shaking his head slowly. "There's rubble enough in my backyard to bury the lot of them." He's staring at my hands. "That's a useful trick."

23

Setting up a lab in the North was no easy thing. I had to install so much infrastructure. You think my labs run on solar power? And I had Lily to consider. She was just a baby. Years passed and I made little progress. And then I met an extraordinary boy whose gift was still evolving; what miracles were yet to be revealed? When Lily fell ill, I almost gave up. If it wasn't for Joshua... I came to believe he would save my daughter's life.

SAIGE, THE CITY

There are no barricades or walls around the wilderness circling the Base. We abandon our baskets and without a torch we stumble into the untamed undergrowth. Bramble bushes fight with long grass and thistle, with heather and raspberry and nettles. We make it to the edge of a stony clearing in the centre of which stands the Base.

The brick house is impossibly tall and wide, dusted by the light of solar lamps planted at even points around the gravelled courtyard. Row after row of dark windows mark each of its ten floors.

Noah, Stace and I crouch down beside a beech tree, strangled by the knotty branches of ivy climbing its lifeless trunk. There is only one path through the foliage, on which are parked ten black solars. Ivy creeps up the walls of the house all the way to the flat roof. Two wide glass doors at the front reflect clouds in the pre-dawn sky.

Three pairs of MAGs patrol the perimeter.

I let out a long shaky breath and shiver. My heart is in my throat. I will never get used to this. Noah's face is still bloody. Stace is too pale, her eyes too dark.

"All those rooms," Stace whispers.

"Dormitories," says Noah. "Must be, to house so many MAGs. I'm guessing the cells are below ground. We should get back now. We know the route well enough."

We start to move just as a light flickers on in a window at the top of the house. The inky black sky is turning grey. A shadow falls across the window as Noah takes my arm.

"Come on," Noah says. "We need to get out of here."

"Wait," I say.

The figure in the window is pulling back the muslins. It's hard to make out their features, but I'm sure it's a woman because she is braiding long pale hair into a single plait, letting it drop against her dark shirt. When she lets go of the curtain and moves back into the room, we exhale.

"Saige," I whisper. "That's *her*."

Giften and Circle are sneaking off the land, fading into the gloomy streets of the City as we emerge from the wilderness.

At midnight tonight, we'll be back. And this time, to fight.

A gust of wind ripples through the trees, and autumn leaves tumble down. The smell of something rotting hits my nose. The stench is thick and sour. Stace buries her face in her elbow.

"Ruthie, no!" Noah hisses as I scramble back through the bushes.

"I want to see where the smell is coming from," I hiss back. A dead body? A dead Giften left to rot after Saige Corentin has finished with them? Graylings. Ottoway. How many more have to die?

Stace is behind me. When I find what I'm looking for, I wish I'd just kept moving.

The foliage has been cut back to make a space for the huge pile of bulging hessian sacks. The same sacks we pack with the Offering.

I stare at the bags spilling their contents of rotting fruit and vegetables; the sour smell fills my nose, thick and decaying. I think I'm going to be sick. I shine my torch onto the decomposing veg, alive with maggots and flies and black beetles. Stace grabs the torch, shutting it off. Not a dead Giften. But the death of something else. A lie that made us keep on filling the sacks.

"This is our food," I tell her, my voice trembling. "They're just letting it rot." I feel like a fool for believing the Offering fed the City folk. Keeping these people and mine on the verge of starvation is the only goal. Because how can hungry people fight?

*　　　*　　　*

"You did what?" Alia is furious and Noah cowers under the twins' gaze. "You didn't stop to think that someone would notice they're missing?"

"You weren't there, Alia," says Stace. "They were disgusting. They had their hands all over me!"

Back in the Tombs it's stuffy and dark and crowded. Alia looms over Noah, her hands on her hips, while he sits cross-legged on the grimy wooden floorboards beside Zan, picking from a plate of food.

"He said they were drinking potato wine," Zan says. "My guess is that it wouldn't be unusual for a couple of drunks to disappear for a bit."

"What should we have done?" Stace throws up her hands. "Should I have gone with them?"

"I'm not saying that," says Alia, huffily, but then she's turning to Noah again. "Did you get smart with them, Noah?"

"That's enough," Zan says. "A couple of stupid MAGs go missing for a day, so what? By tomorrow it's all over in any case."

Gregor joins our group, sinking down next to Zan. "Drunk MAGs, eh?" he says. "Reckon they deserved what was coming to them."

"Let's just hope that old guy can keep his mouth shut," Zan says. "Hungry, desperate people will do anything for food."

"*He* killed one of them!" Stace insists. I put a hand on her arm, but she shrugs me off. "*He* buried them in his yard, he's not going to tell anyone anything."

"You know," I say, taking a plate from the small table laden with food. "Those MAGs weren't in great shape." I think of their bellies straining against their shirts, the stink of liquor on their breath. "Not muscly or tall."

"They'll be the Base staff." Ian has come back to the Tombs for one final meeting with Zan, while the Circle prepares for battle in their own safe houses. He takes a long drink from a leather pouch. "They don't leave the City, generally."

"You know this how?" asks Alia.

"We're the Circle." Ian grins at her. "Eyes. Everywhere. But," he looks at Noah, "that *was* stupid. We were meant to stay invisible. Last thing we need are MAGs patrolling the City looking for their lost sheep."

Noah sets his plate down and stands up, nose to nose with Ian, whose blond spikes are an even brighter yellow in the torchlight.

"That right?" says Noah.

"Yeah." Ian smiles and Noah scowls.

Behind them Gregor lets out a snort of laughter. "Boys," he says. "You're like over-tired smallies. I should send you to bed."

And then the twins are laughing and so is Stace. But Ian and Noah are flushed, agitated, their fingers splayed ready for whatever comes next.

"I could take you," says Ian slowly. He grins.

"I'd kill you before you raised a fist," Noah replies. "Before you even thought about it." But then he's grinning too.

"With one of your pointy arrows?" Ian's eyes sweep the room. "Dev," he calls, "come and settle this, will you? I could take Noah, couldn't I?"

*   *   *

Today has felt like the longest day of my life, but it was also way too short. The Tombs are a cocoon where time has no meaning. The flickering light remains constant and there is no birdsong or blue sky. Everyone is subdued as they eat or clean their weapons. Many tuck knives and short, pointed steel bars into their belts. We make mud in long tubs of dry earth. While Stace and I roll out our mats to get a few hours' sleep before midnight, Zan tells us in detail what she wants us to do.

While this is our battle as much as anyone's, Stace and I won't be fighting. Neither of us is skilled with the bow or with our fists. Instead, we'll be disabling the MAG solars around the Base. Zan beckons Noah over and he nods along as she explains.

And then we follow him outside. The late afternoon sun has turned the clouds into pink cushions in the sky.

"MAGs can't get away if their cars don't work. There'll be no escaping their reckoning," Noah tells us as he rummages beneath the dashboard of Zan's solar. "These wires, see them? Yank hard, pull them right out." He shows us a handful of strands of thin black cable. "Hard, OK? Until they come free. And look for guns, too. Ammo."

*   *   *

And now, Stace holds my hand as we too lie down to try and get some sleep.

"Whatever happens tomorrow, let's stick together, OK?" she says; her face catches strange shadows in the yellow light.

I nod slowly. Tomorrow is just hours away.

As I drift off I think of the war stories from the old books, where battles weren't fought by hand to hand combat but by massive explosions that erupted from the push of a button. I think about zombies and spaceships. Where were the stories of simple farmers and the Giften, forced to become soldiers so they could nurture the land that fed them?

When it's all over, when the MAGs are either dead or captured, I will go into the Base and find my dad and Seb, I think, my eyelids growing heavy. My last thoughts are of Joshie, chasing me and Stace through the Woods one autumn day long ago.

*   *   *

Midnight. In a dark and cloudless sky, a strip of moon lights the long grass in which we stand. This is good and bad. We won't be stumbling around in the dark, but we're not invisible either. Soon, we will head for the Base, but this time it's not to make sure of the route, it's to fight. The Sanctuary gathers in small groups, talking in low voices.

With dawn just hours away, the air smells like the Woods after a day of rain; it's strangely comforting, as is the scrabbling of tiny feet in the bushes. But the distant caw from the odd seagull reminds me that nothing is familiar about this place.

"OK?" Noah asks, shining a torch into my face. He's dressed in MAG black and for the briefest moment I'm disorientated. I look down at my own black clothes. We're all MAGs tonight.

"I'm fine," I say.

Noah's hands have started to feel familiar, I think, as he takes my fingers and lifts them to his cheek. The long scar across the knuckles of one, a missing fingertip on the other. All of it evidence of his life as a Sanctuary soldier. His grey eyes are black in the dark. I can feel the heat coming off his body as he pulls me close. I remember the night I felt so lonely that I might have leaned in to kiss anyone whose face was so close to mine. But as he wraps his arms around me, I let myself sink into his warmth, for just a moment.

"When this is all over, we'll have more time," he says.

But right now, I can't think beyond a single footstep.

"I'm OK. Really," I say, stepping out of his arms. With Stace, we set off through the grass and walk in silence until we're on the same cobbled street of wooden shacks. There is a candle in the window of the old man's house. I can smell potato wine in the air; my boots crunch shards of glass. A smear of black blood on the cobblestones. But we move on, towards a houseful of sleeping MAGs.

24

I'm not a geneticist, but I had help, I made break-throughs; Giften DNA is different, therein lies the secret, the miracle, the revelation. Joshua was the key to long lives, healthy lives, free of pain, free of disease. But I needed more time, Lily was dying. The stem cell therapy failed again and again. Joshua was still changing, you see, the treatment wasn't stable. And in the end, Lily's leukaemia killed her.

SAIGE, THE CITY

My heart is a strip of dried meat in my chest. There's no one about, but shadows move behind thin curtains in dark houses. It feels like the night is holding its breath. The snap of twigs under our feet is swallowed up by the general cacophony of night animals prowling the shrubs and woodland areas of the City.

And now, deep in the wilderness around the Base, Sanctuary and Circle wait, ready to pounce.

But first, the night patrol must die. Zan says this like she might be instructing Noah to tie up the boat, or the twins to light the fire.

Zan, Ian, Dev, the twins, Stace and I are crouching in the spiky bracken. Zan is on her knees, binos focused on three pairs of MAGs slowly walking the perimeter of the gravelled courtyard. The house is dark.

The light from tall solar lamps fixed into the ground along the edge of the wilderness picks out the MAGs' features and the shiny grips of their holstered weapons, as they come and go. Grey clouds move across the sky as heavy boots crunch gravel. Two MAGs draw closer. My nails dig into the flesh of my palms. *Calm down*, I tell myself. *Stay focused*.

"She's always up for it," boasts one, giving the other a playful punch on the arm. "Which is OK by me," he snorts.

"Maybe that's 'cos she's scared of you," says the other, rubbing his arm. He wasn't laughing. "Not my thing, Harry."

"*Not my thing, Harry*," mocks Harry. "What is your *thing*, Dougie?"

They move off, their voices disappearing into the night.

"I'll take Harry," growls Noah.

Zan points at Alia and Noah and then at the bushes on the opposite side of the courtyard. Before they leave Zan catches Noah's sleeve.

"Quick and quiet, OK?"

They edge deeper into the undergrowth.

Zan turns to Ian and points towards the top of the clearing, behind the house. "Take Dev."

I haven't said one word since we entered this stretch of wild land. My heart is thudding louder than the scrabbling of animals in the trees.

Within minutes one set of MAGs has disappeared into the undergrowth. An owl hoots soft and low and then the quick blink from a torch flashes in the trees. Alia and Noah. This is soon followed by another flash from Ian's location; more MAGs down.

The final two, oblivious to the fact that the rest of their patrol isn't following them, move towards our location; *crunch, crunch, crunch*. Harry and Dougie. Harry, the one who likes to frighten women, stops suddenly, taking Dougie's arm. The men stare into the empty courtyard.

"Did they go back in?" Harry asks, but Dougie doesn't reply. He's peering into the bushes. His hand goes to his holster.

My mouth is dry and my body is sticky with cold sweat. I feel Stace's warm breath on my neck.

"I'm scared," she whispers.

I nod my head up and down.

Annis is crouching, ready to pounce. Zan picks up a long branch from the ground and snaps it in half. The MAGs freeze. Harry's drooping cheeks flush. His small, mean eyes narrow as he squints into the bushes, trying to see in the dark. Over his shoulder looms the long thin face of Dougie, fearful, sweaty. Zan snaps the branch in half again and the men startle.

And then they step into the brambles.

I want to cover my face with my hands as Annis and Zan leap, but I don't. Stace and I scoot backwards. They each grab a MAG by the arm and yank the men hard into the undergrowth. Their hands, knees and faces plunge into the thorny, heaving foliage. Annis is on Harry's back in a second and Zan is on top of Dougie. I want to scream. I slap my hands over my mouth. The women push the MAGs' heads into the ground, in sequence, silencing any attempt to cry out. It's clear they've practised these very manoeuvres before. Harry sounds like he's choking on thorns.

Zan is efficient, her dreads tucked away under a black headwrap, her mouth a thin line of determination. She pulls a steel bar from her sleeve, clamps it around Dougie's neck and tugs. He goes silent very quickly.

But Harry is bucking hard. The back of his head skims Annis's mouth and she's thrown off. Zan reaches over, trying to lay a hand on the bare flesh of his saggy cheeks, but Harry is on his feet, stumbling backwards towards the clearing, his hand going for his gun.

He opens his mouth to shout but all that comes out is a thorny croak. Annis wipes blood from her lips; she is unsteady on her feet, moving too slowly. Zan trips in the brambles as she tries to run, landing on her knees.

Harry's hand is on the grip of his weapon when I find myself moving, lunging, the full force of my body slamming into his. I won't let a man like Harry stop us now, we've come too far. He lands on his back, winded. He opens his mouth once more to scream. I forget where I am, who I am. I can't see the bushes, or the others. All I have to do is silence him. I slap my hands over his mouth as he begins to cry out. I press desperation and rage into his flesh. I think of the MAG who couldn't stop leering at Stace. And of the old man who buried a lifetime of hurt into the chest of her attacker.

Harry looks confused and then very afraid. His face is red, he's breathing hard. I take my hands away to watch his lips and cheeks dimple and blister. His eyes begin to close and then they snap open.

"You have no idea what's coming," he croaks before passing out.

Stace, Annis, Zan and I stare at him in silence.

"What did he say?" I whisper.

"Gregious fool." Annis is poking her white hair back under her black headscarf. "Who knows what kind of crazy he is."

But Zan is quiet, her eyes still on the MAG whose final words have unnerved us all. She gets down on her knees, takes his head in her hands and twists. I will never get used to this. The crack of the MAG's neck shoves bile into my throat.

"He was trying to scare us," says Zan, still on her knees, her hands still on the dead man. "Why should we listen to anything that comes out of a MAG's mouth?"

"Even their last words?" I say.

A tight smile forms on Zan's lips. "He didn't know those were his last words, did he?"

The wind moves in the trees, parting branches and leaves to let in the moonlight.

Harry's face, half hidden in the brambles, drips dark blood from a thousand scratches. His eyes are open, wide and glassy. A monster.

"We say nothing about this to the others," Zan says. "It's not enough to stop us, but it might make some nervous."

"Don't worry, Zan," says Annis. "It was just the gibbering nonsense of a burned man."

Noah and Ian appear just as the sound of solar wheels crunching over gravel fills the air.

We crouch low in the bushes once more. The track through the undergrowth is metres away. Doors open and slam shut and four MAGs walk into the light of the courtyard. They move slowly, removing their gloves as they head for the glass doors.

"Lazy drunks," says one. "They'll be back when the liquor's run out."

"But it's the principal," says another. "They were told to hold their positions." He stops and gazes into the empty clearing. "Hang on. Where's the patrol?" They all stop, their heads moving left and right.

"Probably getting drunk too." Laughter fills the clearing. They head for the house, but the last MAG in the line pauses before entering. He sweeps his torch into the undergrowth for long moments before he disappears inside.

"They're spooked," says Zan. "It's not good."

"In ten minutes they'll be in bed," Ian says softly. "Then the first wave."

I take Stace's hot hand in mine. The others are on their feet, but we stay low.

The *first wave*—fifty fighters will enter the Base and draw the battle into the courtyard, when the second wave of another fifty will charge. And then the third and more until the fight is over.

"Ruthie, that MAG. Do you think…?" Stace's words die on her tongue as the faces of Circle and Sanctuary appear at the edges of the undergrowth, where they wait.

Zan crouches low as she pads slowly across the gravel. My heart hammers a drum beat as she levers off the handle with a thin steel bar she has pulled from her belt, and the glass doors of the Base swing open. She turns and makes a circling motion in the air with her hand. The first wave emerges from the wilderness and starts to run.

25

Lily died, but she's not dead. I have come to believe in miracles. Science is merely a tool, a microscope, a lens through which to view the heavens.

SAIGE, THE CITY

ne hundred feet hit the gravel. In twos and threes they follow Zan through the open doors. There's a moment or two of complete quiet. And then it starts.

The glass doors shatter in their frames as a shriek of bullets rips the silence apart. Flashes of gunfire blink into the darkness. Lights flick on in dark windows. All I can hear from the house are gunshots and grunts and crashing furniture.

When the fight spills out into the courtyard my heart sinks.

"They're in their *uniforms!*" Stace gasps. She is squeezing my arm too hard.

They should have been asleep, yet here they are, dressed, armed with bludgeons and guns. They even have gloves on.

The courtyard is a blur of bodies in motion, but there aren't even fifty MAGs here.

"Where are the rest?" breathes Stace. "Ian said *six hundred*."

"Stace, we need to do our job," I say. I hear the panic in my voice. Something is definitely wrong. The night air seems to close around us, a suffocating blanket. "Come on."

We edge through a wilderness of brambles and nettles and weeds and long grass; it's slow progress in the dark, even with our wind-up torches.

"Ruthie," Stace catches my arm. "Look!" We're almost on the path lined with black solars, but we pause to stare into the courtyard.

Circle on MAG, Giften on MAG. No guns any more; this is hand to hand combat. Knives glint in the solar light. I watch Noah stab a MAG in the neck with a hunting knife; a long stream of blood spurts from the wound, into Noah's face, sinking into the black fabric of his shirt. He turns around and plunges his knife into the chest of another. Annis sits astride the shoulders of a squat, heavy MAG, her fingers pressed deep into his eyes as he screams. She leaps off him as he sinks to his knees, hands over his face, blood pouring from between his fingers. Alia ducks and spins at the edge of the action, loading her bow with arrows, as she takes aim and fires. It is a nightmare, playing out before our eyes. Is this what I imagined the fight would look like? I keep breathing. In and out. In and out.

Zan is punching, spinning, smashing, kicking and *burning* MAGs as she twirls through the writhing, screaming mob. She is electrifying.

Dev picks up a MAG and throws him into the undergrowth. The MAG starts to crawl away, but Alia's arrow whizzes past Dev's ear into the man's neck. Ian drives a knife into the back of another who is charging at Dev with a bludgeon. He and Ian slap palms in the air.

A scramble in the bushes and the second wave streams past us into the clearing.

"Into the house," shouts Zan and they run through the doors.

Stace is tugging on my sleeve. "I can't... let's just do our thing."

We find the cars and one by one I yank the fine wires free of their moorings, while Stace searches the boots for weapons. When we emerge she is empty-handed.

"No guns," she says. "Nothing."

From above, a sudden crack of bullets flies into the courtyard and we fall to our knees in the undergrowth, covering our heads with our hands. At the edge of the courtyard we have a clear view of the house. I look up to see a bare-chested MAG hovering at an upper window, firing his gun into the crowd below, hitting MAGs and non-MAGs alike. His gun clicks empty and he disappears inside, but then he's back, shooting again. *Everyone* ducks, covering their heads, running for the bushes. But then another figure appears behind him. This is how we lose,

I think, picturing an armed MAG at every window of the Base. Picked off, one by one.

But it's not a MAG, it's Noah. He smashes a steel pipe into the back of the shooter's head. The MAG doubles over, his torso flops out of the window. Noah grabs his legs and launches the rest of him into the night air. We watch him land hard, in a splash of red. Giften, MAGs and Circle scatter. And then they're back into the fight.

The Giften look like they're dancing as they take down the MAGs, their movements fluid, controlled, sharp and precise. The Circle is brutal, ripping open bellies with swipes of their long knives.

The fight is almost over. There are no more wild bellows of rage from either side. Just the thump of fists on flesh, the cracking of bones as metal sticks are hammered into skulls and legs and arms and backs.

"It can't be this easy," says Stace. "Where are the rest of them?"

You have no idea what's coming.

"That MAG…" I say. "Do you think…?"

"I don't know. I don't know!" Stace is on her feet, edging towards the courtyard, but she springs back as more gunshots burst into the clearing from inside the house.

MAGs charge outside, chased by the second wave. But there can't be more than twenty of them. They're struck down by Alia's arrows as they run for the undergrowth.

And then it's really over.

It's as if the night is exhaling; a dusty, heavy silence falls over the courtyard and the wilderness beyond—even the nocturnal creatures have paused in their hunt for food.

Bodies scatter the gravel. Hundreds of baffled Circle and Sanctuary faces appear at the edges of the wilderness.

"Let's go." I can't manage more than a whisper. I'm sweating and freezing at once. My legs shake as we make our way across the courtyard.

Something is very wrong.

*   *   *

A large glass ball of solar light hangs from the high ceiling in the main room, emitting a low glow. Black and white stone tiles cover the floor and an expansive staircase sweeps up one side of the room, curving around the pale yellow walls. For an insane moment I wonder if Filip could make such a set of stairs.

There are more bodies in here.

Circle and Sanctuary gather to form a circle around Ian and Zan; the fighters catching their breath, faces and hands bruised and bloody.

No one is celebrating.

"Zan!" I push through the crowd; uncomfortably aware I don't have a scratch on me. "We have to tell them," I say.

Zan has cuts to her face and arms. She's breathing fast. The room falls silent around us as Zan raises an arm. I open my mouth to speak Harry's last words, but her hand drops to my shoulder, silencing me too.

"It's OK, Ruthie," she says.

The crowd closes in.

"It's obvious to everyone by now that they knew we were coming," says Zan. She points to the courtyard beyond the smashed glass doors. "There's barely a hundred MAGs out there."

I can feel the room tense. Giften and Circle exchange looks.

"One of the MAGs on patrol said something strange, something I thought at the time meant nothing. But now…" Zan turns to face the dead in the courtyard.

"What did he say?" Gregor booms.

"*You have no idea what's coming*. I thought he was trying to scare us before he died. Now I know it was a warning. This isn't over and maybe it hasn't even started. If I know MAGs, they're out there, waiting for us to lower our guard, to believe we've won."

"And there were no extra guns or ammo in the solars," says Stace.

"Right," Ian calls from the doorway, and every head pivots. "We need to comb every inch of this house and the land around the Base," he says. "We haven't come this far for nothing. Every single stinking MAG will feel our fury." Heads nod up and down in the crowd. "Every single MAG will have to pay for Graylings. For Ottoway." People call out *Aye* and *Let's go* and *One fight!*

The vibration and smell of gunfire is still thick in the air, dead MAGs carpet the courtyard. Were they just sacrifices? Was it their job to exhaust our fighters?

Stace nudges me and together we watch Dev break away from the crowd and disappear through a blue door at the back of the vast room.

The room empties as Ian leads everyone back out into the courtyard. They lift guns from dead bodies, scattered knives. They collect fallen arrows and steel pipes.

Zan sprints up the stairs with Gregor. Her search for Saige Corentin has begun. From outside I hear instructions being shouted, footsteps running across the gravel, the shuffle of leaves as bushes are parted; the search for the missing MAGs is also on. Stace and I stand in the middle of the aftermath of this half-fight. What do we do? Go back into the wilderness and wait? Return to the Tombs?

"Ruthie!" Dev, sweaty, his short hair matted with dust and blood, steps through the blue door. There are cuts to his face and arms. He shoves his gun into the back of his waistband.

"Cells. Downstairs." He's breathless, excited. Dad! I look at Stace and we start forward, but he holds up his hands. "Hang on. Dan's not there. Just Giften. But they might know something." My heart sinks, but at least we're moving.

He pulls open the door and starts down a dark winding staircase.

"Dev, wait!" I say, at the top of the stairs, and point at the courtyard. "What about the fight? Aren't you supposed to be—"

"Right now, I *need* to help you find Dan. And then I need to get you both to safety."

"And Seb? Is he down there?" I ask as the door swings shut behind us, plunging us into darkness.

"No. He's not." At the foot of the stairs, Dev pauses before pushing open another door; Stace stumbles into him. "These people," he whispers, "they're scared, really scared. They heard everything."

We step into a large white room. Bright light pours from tiny points in the ceiling. There are no shadowy corners. Everything glows. Three glass-fronted identical cubes face three others. A narrow corridor runs up the centre of the room, leading to a large red door and a long cupboard on the far wall.

I never once asked Dad what it was like in the cells. The prisons in the old books are dark, stinking places, with jagged rock walls leaking brown ooze and rusting iron rods sunk deep into the ceiling and floor; if anything, I imagined the cells might look more like the Tombs than the room I'm standing in right now. But they *are* cells, it's obvious, even to me, despite their pristine order and cleanliness, because each space contains a mattress and a sink and the doors are sealed.

Five thin, frightened and very pale faces peer at us from behind thick glass. The sixth prisoner is asleep.

The girl in the first cell is young. Her hands hang by her sides, they are bruised and bleeding, as if she too has just been fighting, her eyes dull yellow. My panic becomes dread.

"How do we get you out?" asks Stace.

The girl points to a black square panel set in the wall beside her cell, with three rows of numbers.

"The numbers. It's a code. I don't know mine."

We all stare at the panel, as if staring alone could open these doors. I'm impatient to ask about Dad, to get back upstairs, to look for him. But Dev's face slows me down. He looks heartbroken. The figures could be ghosts. I take a deep breath, just as the boy in the cell behind us thumps the glass.

He is just as thin as the girl; his face long and gaunt. Mousy hair lies flat and greasy on his scalp. Purple circles under his eyes. His hands are also bloody, showing scabs at the tip of each finger.

"I know Rachel's," he says hoarsely. "It's seven-one-seven-one."

"And I know Jonathan's," says Rachel.

One by one, the prisoners reveal the codes, but there's no one to tell us the code for the fifth cell, because the Giften inside cell six is not asleep, but dead. Dev tries pressing random numbers. Nothing happens.

I inspect the keypad in the bright light and notice that the numbers four, eight, five and seven look shinier than the rest.

"It's these numbers," I say. I start tapping in sequences until finally the door slides open.

And there they stand. Five half-starved, bruised and terrified Giften. The room is silent as we take in their sores, the bare patches on their heads, their shrunken bodies.

"Did you come to rescue us?" asks Jonathan.

Something inside me twists. "We did," I say. "But we also need *your* help."

Rachel clicks open the cupboards beside the red door, and pulls out jeans and sweaters, boots. She pauses, to catch her breath, while the others wait, their hands twisting in the thin folds of their nightshirts.

"You need to leave. Right now. The fight isn't over," I say. "But my dad is a prisoner somewhere inside the Base." I try to keep the panic out of my voice. "I don't know where."

"There are other cells," Rachel says, pulling on her boots. "Underground. You need to find the hidden door in the brickwork outside. Saige took me down there and told me to choose which prison I preferred."

"Is there a boy called Joshie here?" Stace asks when they are finished dressing. "He was taken from our community. About five years ago." But they only shake their heads.

*   *   *

Back in the main hall, the ghostly Giften pause, staring around the room at all the dead.

"Go outside," says Rachel. "Turn left and left. The door is under a brass symbol of a hand." She grimaces. "Saige's little joke." A distant memory tugs my thoughts as I watch them head out of the Base and into the night.

This house doesn't creak in the wind like my cabin. A light breeze blows through the open doors to stir up dust. It swirls around our feet and then falls back to the ground. The sky is getting lighter because now I can see into the corners of this room and there is nothing to be scared of in any of them.

We hear the pounding of feet above our heads, doors slamming shut, Zan cursing.

Gregor appears on the landing. "She's not up here," he says.

*   *   *

The air outside is still heavy with the stink of sweat, blood and gunfire. Flashes of torchlight prick the dark of the undergrowth. Hesitant birdsong heralds the dawn. A few days ago I was on an island in the sea, before that I was in a circle of land in the middle of a vast forest. Where am I now?

I need a minute.

I cross the courtyard and at the edge of the wilderness, I shove away weeds and brambles until my hands find the earth. The tension eases instantly. If I feel stronger, then I'll find Dad, I'll find Seb; we'll win, I bargain.

"Come *on*!" yells Dev into the half-light. "The door's right here."

Wiping mud off my hands I head back across the clearing to where Dev stands with Stace before a door carved out of the brickwork. Above it the palm of a hand, fingers spread wide, is embossed onto a dull yellow brass plate. I remember Saige's copper brooch.

And then the air erupts.

26

*Like all Giften, Joshua had the power to nurture
arid wastelands into abundant forests. But he could
also do so much more. Beyond the gift of life, he had
death in his fingers.*

SAIGE, THE CITY

right light floods the courtyard, as though the
sun has been switched on by a mighty hand. Solar
lamps beam from the roof of the Base into the
wilderness. The bushes tremble as figures begin to stream
through the trees. We're frozen in place, unable to look
away as MAGs, wielding bludgeons and guns, stomp their
way towards the courtyard. Hundreds of them. Giften and
Circle steam forward to meet them.

"There's so many of them," breathes Stace.

"There's many of us too." Dev, the first of us to come to
his senses, pushes against the heavy door with new urgency.
"I need to get you inside, safe, then I'm coming back."

The door starts to creak open.

Dev catches my arm as I follow Stace into another dark
space. "Wait!" he gasps, turning around. "Over there!"

The courtyard is a scrum. This is a real battle. Curses and grunts fill the air. Guns abandoned once more, knives glint in the bright light. The air sings with violence. But Dev isn't watching the fighters. He's looking beyond them, at the men and women pouring through the undergrowth. In the rough patchwork clothes of the communities, they carry weapons fashioned from shovels and shears and rakes and forks. Tools that were once used to raise food from the earth are now instruments of vengeance.

These are *my* people. The farmers. The *communities*.

And running ahead of them, leading the way with a fist in the air, in a familiar dust-coloured coat, is the Recorder.

"Logan," I breathe.

But then Dev is pushing Stace and I into the dark.

My heart hammers as we climb down jagged stones jutting out of the wall, a sheer drop on the other side. Stace is breathing hard, firing questions none of us can answer. Did Logan bring the communities? Did I see her father? Owen?

Instead of the flaming torches of the Tombs, solar lamps light our descent. The thick cloying smell of damp earth and shit fills my mouth and nose. I'm in another underground room.

The walls are rough stone blocks, fitted together in uneven, craggy rows. Yellow streaks trace lines where streams of water run down their rocky surface, like tiny, polluted rivers.

This is a prison from the old stories of torture and dungeons. Dark and brutal. A splash of colour catches my eye; there is a narrow door in the brickwork, painted bright green, opposite the staircase.

We step onto an earth floor, muddy where the water has pooled. Dull yellow light pours from tiny bulbs fixed to the wooden beams overhead. Fat rats race between iron bars gnarled with rust from the constant dripping. There are two rows of three cells, a wide walkway between them.

"Stace!" I reach for her hand. I see him!

In the cell at the end of a row, Dad's thin brown fingers wrap the bars, his face appears between the gaps.

"Ruthie, for the love of the land!"

I race down the room, skidding in the mud.

My father is bruised, both eyes swollen and black; but he's still alive, he's still Dad.

"I came to find you," I pant, my hands reaching for his. "I had to find you." I think everything will be fine. The battle will be won and I can take Dad back to the Field. But Dad doesn't look relieved to see us.

"You can't be here! None of you! How did you even…?" He takes a deep breath and looks at Dev. "Outside, tell me," he says. "The fighting."

"Logan's here, Dan. With the communities," says Dev. "The Sanctuary too."

"The Sanctuary?" His voice is hoarse, unsteady. "They're fighting *with* the Circle?" Dad stands up straighter. A little hope has come into his eyes.

"It was Ruthie, Dan. She brought the Sanctuary and the Circle together." Dev is grinning, but he's also backing away. "I need to get out there. After… afterwards I'll come back for you."

And then a voice cracks the air inside this cavernous underground dungeon. I know this voice. I've heard it before, awake and in my nightmares. It's shrill, mean and absolutely sure of itself.

"No one is going anywhere!"

Saige Corentin. How long has she been standing there? A cold hand closes around my heart.

"Dear God," whispers Dad.

I turn around slowly to see her standing in front of the green door. She is flanked by two MAGs.

From the corner of my eyes, a blur of motion, and Dev is aiming his gun at Saige.

"Drop it!" screams one MAG. He is even taller than Dev.

But Dev is edging forward, the muscles in his arms tense.

"Dev!" I whisper. "Don't!"

"Listen to her, Dev," Saige Corentin's sickly sweet voice coaxes.

The giant MAG fires at the ceiling, wood splinters pop and fall. And Dev very slowly lays down the gun and holds up his hands.

I can hear the others breathing hard, just like me. The sound of the bullet rings in my head, but then other sounds too. The fighting outside. It comes and goes in waves as it draws closer and moves away. This is how it ends. For me anyway. And for Dad and Dev and Stace. Zan might win this battle yet, but it will be too late for us. I've seen with my own eyes what Saige does to those who stand in her way. My breath slows. Is this what dying feels like? I think of Mum and Ant. Of the Field. I hope it's fast.

A MAG is walking towards us now. He has a doughy, bright red face, dripping; the Giant covers him, sweeping his weapon back and forth. Red Beard's neck is exactly the same width as his head, I notice, stupidly. He picks up Dev's gun and shoves it into his belt.

"I'm going to pat you down," he barks. His hands are rough as he moves them over my body. He takes Dev's knives and Stace's gun.

Saige Corentin's boots squelch in the mud as she approaches. Her hair is long and yellow, pulled into a high ponytail. She's old, but not as old as Jacintha or Lucia. She has cold blue eyes and flushed, freckled cheeks; she looks like she's been slapped. Her mouth is mean even now when she's smiling. I try hard to feel fear or even anger, but I only feel numb.

"You have lost," Dad growls, his knuckles tight around the bars. "The Base is ours. Everyone in the North who hates you is fighting now. You're trapped."

She cocks her head towards the stairs, towards the sounds of battle. "I don't think this is over yet, *Dan*." She laughs, but it's not a happy sound. It's cruel and mocking. I feel a shiver travel up my damp spine.

In my mind and after all these years she had become a myth, an ogre, but she is really just a flesh and blood woman. The MAGs share the same mocking leer on their faces. The Giant is eerily familiar.

"Enjoy this moment while you still can," Dev growls under his breath. "There's nowhere you can go."

"You're the one at gunpoint, boy. Do I look trapped to you?" She cups a hand to her ear. "Keep listening. You kill a few of my men and stand here telling me *I've lost my house?*" She yells the final words. Her voice jolts me out of my trance. It's like being screamed at by a dragon.

The Giant pulls a large rusty key from his shirt pocket which he shoves into the lock of Dad's cell, and one by one we're pushed inside.

Saige comes closer; the MAGs at her back. She doesn't say anything for a long time. She has fine lines around her eyes and mouth, but her skin is too smooth; she hasn't spent a minute working the land in the sun, snow and rain. She wears a thick white cotton shirt and loose white trousers. The only colour, aside from her pink cheeks, are the shiny red boots on her feet.

"You're the traitor's daughter," she says to me. "Did you come to rescue him?"

Dad steps in front of me. "She's just a kid who's got caught up in something she doesn't understand. She's not a threat to you."

"Really? And yet here she is, the Sanctuary at her beck and call, killing my men. Stand aside, Dan."

The Giant points his gun at Dad, who doesn't move.

"You know, they say that ambition is in the blood," she says. "So if you're anything like your father, you will have inherited his singular desire to destroy me. And my work." She turns to the Giant. "Kill her."

"No!" Stace stands beside Dad. But it's futile. If she wants to kill me, they can't stop her and there's nowhere left to run.

"She is Giften." Dad's voice is thick, choked. "Giften."

I step away from Dad and Stace, in full view of Saige once more, who smiles. I won't let her kill them to save myself. I won't show her my fear. The last thing she will see on my face is defiance.

"I have Giften," she says. "And when this is over, I'll have my pick of the Sanctuary."

The Giant MAG raises his gun, but Dad is lunging for me.

Heat fills my body, from my feet to the top of my head. My hands are on fire. Dad fingers close around mine, as he starts to drag me towards the back of the cell.

"Let go of me, Dad!" I scream. "I don't want to hurt you!" I yank free and inspect my burning hands. I show him my palms. "Don't come near me." Silence hangs in the air like someone just switched off a storm.

I turn around to face Saige once more. I'm going to bet everything on this woman's hunger for Giften.

"I am more than Giften," I tell her. "I can *burn*."

27

If Joshua could kill another human being by touch alone, might he also not be able to do the very opposite? Give life to the dead? Might he not, one day, bring Lily back? But killing even the smallest creature took its toll on the boy and we had such a long way to go. He became ill himself. I had pushed him too hard, desperate for results.

SAIGE, THE CITY

"Now *that* is interesting." Saige Corentin pushes aside the Giant's gun. She draws closer, and so do I. And then another smell fills my nose; it's her scent. It shields the putrid stink of shit and decay with something more fragrant. *Of course*, she's wearing essence of lavender. I'm instantly back at Graylings. Dead and bloated bodies rear up in my mind, while bile rises in my throat.

"Ruthie," warns Stace as I raise my hands to the bars. "Don't."

She is right. I can't reach Saige anyway.

"You are angry," she says, a smile pushing up the corners of her mouth. "And anger makes *you* dangerous—"

The sound of hammering on the heavy door at the top of the stone steps cuts her off.

"Ralph! Colin!" a male voice booms.

The Giant and Red Beard charge up the stairs. The noise of fighting gets louder for the few seconds the door is open. Feet running on the gravel, shouting and yelling, the wet thumps of fists on flesh. The door is slammed shut, locked and bolted.

The MAGs jog back down the stairs.

"Report?" Saige asks.

"A lot of dead, doctor," says Red Beard. "We've lost a lot of men. But we're winning. No doubt about that."

"They were already knackered. It's just a matter of finishing them off." The Giant is looking at Dev, his mouth a sneer of pure loathing.

"You knew we were coming." Dev comes up to the bars, his hands curled into fists at his sides. "Didn't you?" He's sweating, furious.

Saige stares at him for a long moment. "Did I know the Sanctuary and the Circle were going to join forces and try to bring down the Base? Is that what you're asking?" None of us moves. "Bring them in," she instructs the MAGs. "It's time for a reunion."

The Giant nods and heads for the green door.

The hot ball in my stomach starts to cool as I let myself, for a moment or two, forget where I am and who is holding me captive. In my father's prison cell, I sink to my knees and push my fingers into the soft damp earth.

I need my wits, and even here, in these rooms of torture and death, the soil wants to speak to me.

Green shoots sprout beneath my fingers. I tug them free and hold them to my nose. Instead of lavender and animal droppings, I inhale the smell of life.

"You, girl," Saige says, but I don't look up.

A different kind of heat fills my body now. I think of the Blazes, where for hours at a time I nurtured an incinerated landscape to raise pumpkins and wild garlic, beans and yellow onions.

"I want to help you, show you your potential."

I brush the dirt from my fingers and stand. A burst of gunfire from above. In the old stories, I'd be out there fighting with the others, *burning*. Stace would ride a magnificent horse, while slicing a sword through the air. Dad would be the hero. But instead, we're in a dungeon, caged and powerless to do anything but listen to our friends die.

"They say you're trying to share the gift," I say, ignoring her offer of help. "They say you want everyone to become Giften. That you take us apart to make everyone else *better*. So which is it? Do you want to show me my potential or do you want to kill me?" The earth has calmed me, just as it always does. I feel the soil under my nails, in the crevices of my palms.

There is silence in the room. Red Beard shuffles from foot to foot as if he's bored, as if he'd rather be out there, fighting and killing.

Saige sighs, and pulls her ponytail tight. "It's not that simple, traitor's daughter. If you let me just show—"

"My name is Ruthie," I tell her.

"Ruthie, you can *burn*. You can necrotize. You are prematurely ageing your enemies, did you know that? Of course you didn't." She gives a tight smile. Red Beard flinches at the word *enemies*. "But it's the stage beyond *burning* that drives my work. This is where I can show you miracles." Her eyes drift to the wall behind me. "I've only encountered such a phenomenon once."

"Encountered *what*?" I ask, despite myself. Once again, Saige begins to pace the walkway between the cells.

"Ruthie!" Dad moves to my side, his hand on my arm. "You don't need to hear her lies."

"Not lies, Dan. This boy was my finest Giften." She says this more to herself than to Dad. "I picked him up myself. In fact," she looks at Dad, "you were there. Don't you remember?" She stops pacing and shoots me a hateful look. "Tell me, *Ruthie*. What is so special about the Field that it delivers such *prizes*?"

Dev lunges through the bars, snatching at the air as he tries to grab Saige. Dad pulls him away and Red Beard lifts his gun.

"Dev!" Dad says. "Get hold of yourself!"

"But it's Joshie!" Dev's voice is husky with rage. "She's talking about Joshie." He looks at the woman in white, his teeth bared, like he wants to bite her. "Where is he? What have you done to him?"

Saige opens her mouth to answer as the green door opens and the Giant steps through, followed by Owen.

And Seb.

28

I woke up one morning to find a trail of dead men from Joshua's cell to the wilderness. He was gone.

SAIGE, THE CITY

For a single moment I don't register Owen at all, because here is Seb. Alive and safe.

And then my insides feel like they're shrinking, like someone is tying my guts into knots, then kicking me hard in the stomach. Saige Corentin lays an arm across Seb's shoulders, and he turns to *smile at her,* sliding his hands into his spotless, white trouser pockets.

"Seb?" Stace and I say at the same time.

It can't be him. It doesn't make sense. For a second, I wonder if he has a twin. A brother on the wrong side.

The smile dries on his lips. Seb isn't a prisoner. He isn't even hurt.

"What did they...?" I begin, but my heart is thumping in my throat, in my head. Why is he letting Saige *touch* him?

"You're a gregious traitor!" gasps Dev. His voice bounces off the rock walls as his hands curl around the iron bars. He's gulping air, as if he's just taken another punch in the gut. "You betrayed us? Your people?"

"Dev!" Stace yells. "Stop it! It's Seb."

"You… you… you—" A vein throbs at Dev's temple.

"*You you you*," mimics Seb, stepping away from Saige and up to the bars. He rears back as Dev's arms shoot through, fingers reaching. "Steady, Dev," Seb says. "You're not a hero any more. You're not even a soldier." He blows strands of white hair out of his eyes. "You were so desperate to join the Circle, weren't you? So desperate to make people like *me* look bad for wanting to live a simple life. But look at where you are now." He pauses to laugh. "And where I am."

"Seb?" Tears begin to fall down Stace's cheeks. She doesn't wipe them away. I look at him, at the smirk on his mouth. He doesn't deserve her tears.

"Stop crying, Stace," I tell her. I nod towards Owen, who is smiling through his black beard. "There's no point. He's the one behind this."

"Ruthie," Owen says, gesturing at the surroundings. "Happy now?"

My stomach lurches.

"Dad," snaps Seb. "This isn't her fault. I told you already. It's all Dan."

"My mum…" I say, fighting to control my voice. "She'll kill you, she'll—"

"She'll *thank* me for bringing back your body. Poor Ruthie, another victim of the senseless fighting."

The urge to lay my throbbing fingers on his flesh is choking me.

"Dad!" Seb barks. "No one is dying! Ruthie will come round. They all will."

"Was this your plan all along?" Stace is at the bars now; her tears have vanished, replaced by rage. It is a burning arrow aimed at the boy she once loved. "Is that why you came with us? Just to report back to *him*?"

"This young man is the hero of the hour. And his father is my new Captain of the Base." Saige is enjoying our pain. "If it wasn't for Seb and his uncanny ability to transform himself into a pathetic foot soldier of the Sanctuary, I would never have had the time to prepare this wonderful reception."

"The ambush," Stace says, "was that your doing too?" She's looking at Owen. "You have *poisoned* him against us."

"The MAGs were tracking you, Stace," Dev says, dully. "It's obvious. Following *him*."

"Enough," says Saige. "Seb works for *me*. That's all you need to know."

There is a long minute of silence. Dev, Stace and I stare at our friend and he stares back, the infuriating smile is back on his lips.

"You've been a MAG all this time," says Dad quietly, to Owen. "Haven't you?"

"Well, before that I was a Rover." Owen snorts. "But to you I was a grieving father who'd lost his One and Only on the road. Would you have taken me in otherwise?" Threads begin to weave together in my mind. Owen came to the Field when Seb was just a smallie. We believed all his lies. So did Mum.

"Is Seb your real son?" Dad slams the bars with both fists. "He doesn't even look like you. What did you do? Steal someone's kid? Just so we'd take pity on you? Let you in?"

"Who can resist a grieving father?" says Owen, laying an arm across Seb's shoulders.

"*You* think you're revealing secrets, Dan," snarls Seb, "but you're not. I know who I am. Owen might not be my real dad, but he *rescued* me all the same. And then I rescued him right back. And he's right, you would never have taken in a lone Rover."

"Well, now that we're sharing, I guess it should all come out," says Owen, grinning.

"You don't need to say it," hisses Dad. "Joshie, my kidnap, this ambush—it's all you."

I slide down the bars on to my knees. The tips of my fingers ache as if they've been cut open with a sharp knife. Owen, now he's begun, won't stop talking. The Circle is no better than the Rovers, the Sanctuary is lawless. Only the MAGs can keep order, protect the communities. Under his rule everything will settle down. Especially now, now that we've been defeated.

"What's wrong with you?" Stace's voice slices the air, silencing Owen. She hasn't taken her eyes off Seb since he walked in.

"With me?" Seb points at himself and then at her. "It's your precious Circle that's crazy." He turns to me, hunched on the ground. "We could have gone home after Dan was taken, but you kept on, didn't you, Ruthie? You had to meet the Circle and then the Sanctuary. You know the Circle killed fifty Giften for *nothing*, right? And *I'm* the one that's crazy? Just accept you've lost and move on, for the love of the land, Ruthie."

Angry voices outside, bodies slamming into the ground.

"Do you hear that, Seb?" I say, rising to my feet. I point to the ceiling. "It doesn't sound to me like the fight is over yet."

"That's enough!" shrieks Saige. "It *is* over. Any minute—"

Fists pound on the green door. The Giant moves fast, gun raised, and pulls it open slowly, aiming his weapon into the gap. A MAG appears, breathing hard, his black shirt is torn, there are red gashes on his face and arms, a pool of blood in one ear. But it's the familiar figure he's dragging behind him that makes my heart skid.

It's Logan. Blindfolded.

"The Recorder?" Saige says, stepping aside.

"You see, Dad?" says Seb, snorting. "Not so impartial. Right in the gregious thick of it. Like I told you."

On hands and knees, Logan is no longer wearing the long coat.

"He... or she led the communities in, doctor," the MAG says, ripping off the blindfold.

Thin and filthy the Recorder raises shining, defiant eyes to Saige Corentin.

"*And* the City," the MAG adds, but once the words are out of his mouth he cowers. I too might want to shoot this messenger if I was Saige.

"Get out!" she screams at the MAG. Saige looms over Logan, her hands on her hips, like a mother about to scold a smallie. "You!" she says, her rage building with each word that comes out of her mouth. "You and your poisonous lies. And now you've set my own City against me?"

I bang on the bars until she turns around.

"*You did this.* You've been *starving* your own people," I say. "I found our Offerings rotting in the bushes."

"You have no idea what it takes to rule." Her voice is suddenly icy. "They're as bad as the rest of you; their foul voices forever complaining. People can either eat or fight. They can't do both." She turns back to Logan.

"I've always been curious, Logan. What are you? A man or a woman?"

"I prefer the moniker of Recorder," says Logan, smiling. "Neither one thing nor the other. It seems to help with the work." Logan stands up slowly, face to face with Saige. "But I am a woman. Just like you."

The Giant MAG grabs Logan's arm and pulls her close.

"Doesn't smell like a woman," he says, laughing. "Shall I lock her up with the rest?"

"You see the communities as weak, isolated people." Logan is being dragged towards our cell. "But with nothing more than farm tools and passion we will defeat you. How does that feel?"

Saige's face twists with loathing. "You believe change is born from revolution, Logan, but revolution just makes new dictators. If anything happens to me, prepare yourselves," she spits.

The second the key turns in the lock of the cell door, the wooden door above begins to splinter. Someone is breaking it down. *Our* people are breaking it down.

Saige looks around the room with wild eyes.

"Change of plan," she announces through gritted teeth. "Get them out of there."

Released from the cell I take Logan's hand as we're led across the room. Red Beard, gun aimed at Dad at the front of the line, takes careful backward steps towards the green door. A bubble of hope forms in my chest. I catch Stace's eye. She feels it too.

The Giant brings up the rear, while Owen and Seb and Saige stand to one side, the audience to our procession. I let go of Logan. My hands are hot again. The hammering at the top of the stairs stops and starts, stops and starts.

And then time seems to stop as Owen raises his gun. "We don't need *her*."

He aims at the Recorder, who, in a burst of red and a thundering *bang*, drops to the floor.

I jump back, stumbling into Dad, who is reaching across me to catch Logan, but Red Beard presses his gun into Dad's shoulder.

"Dad!" I scream and he freezes.

The Giant fires at the ceiling as Dev and Stace start towards Logan. Seb and Saige haven't moved. Open-mouthed they can't look away from Owen. Saige is realizing, and I'm glad, that she has no control over this brute.

"You've had your fun." His eyes lock with mine. "Your big adventure is over, Ruthie, and now it's time for the adults to take over." Owen glances towards the door at the top of the stairs and scowls. This is the Owen who has been hiding from me and Mum, from everyone in the Field, ever since he joined us. Here he stands, a mountain of hate; solid, immovable and hard.

I fall to my knees. Logan's warm blood covers my hands as I push them against a seeping hole to staunch the flow, wishing my fingers had the power to heal. Saige has found her voice and is yelling at Owen to stand down, that they need to get out of here.

I feel Logan's heartbeat flicker beneath my fingers. And then it stops. I cover my face with bloody hands.

"I'm not sure we need her either." Owen turns to me, his voice booming above the others.

I look into the eyes of Ant's father, Seb's dad, my mother's One and Only. And I see contempt. I see the barrel of his gun.

"No! I need her!" Saige's voice is shrill, but it has no effect on Owen.

The battering on the door becomes frantic. Owen's finger is on the trigger. A blur of bodies as Dad and

Seb begin to move. The crack of a bullet cuts through the air.

I wait for the thud of a lead ball to hit my body. But it's Seb who goes down. Not me. Not Dad.

Owen drops the gun, his mouth a wide O. I scramble to my feet, as Seb collapses on top of Logan.

Dad elbows Red Beard hard in the throat. The MAG hits the ground, clutching his neck, choking. The Giant's gun clicks empty as he fires at Dad, and then Dev charges.

Dad scrabbles on the ground for Owen's gun, while Owen claws at the blood pumping from Seb's thigh, slowly turning the white cloth of his trousers red.

Another gunshot and a perfectly round red hole appears in the middle of Owen's forehead. Like a felled tree he drops hard and heavy across Seb's body.

Now Dad aims the gun at Red Beard and pulls the trigger.

From another planet I watch Saige escape Dad's third bullet as she charges through the green door.

Dev and the Giant fight in the mud. Dad raises his gun but I catch his arm. The Giant is mine.

This is the MAG who broke Joshie's nose before he pushed him into the back of the black solar. He tied his wrists with a thin cord, so tight it cut into the flesh. He hurt Joshie and now I need to hurt him. I grab the Giant's arm as he raises his fist to Dev and, covered in Logan's blood, I press my loathing into his damp flesh.

He looks at me, his face monstrous, wild. His arm hovers in the air.

"You gregious *freak*. Don't touch me!" he screams.

But I don't let go. He opens his mouth to say more but the light snaps out in his eyes and he falls onto his face.

Stace has dragged Seb away from the lifeless bodies of Owen and Logan. He takes short, fitful breaths. The blood is still pumping from his leg. He is as white as paper. His eyes are open, fixed to the ceiling, sightless. Stace holds his hand.

"Stace, we have to get out of here!" I say.

But she's holding Seb's hand. "He's dying, Ruthie," she whispers.

"Ruthie?" Seb's voice is low, husky. "I never lied about loving you." He's squeezing his eyes open and shut, trying to focus on Stace's face. "Ruthie? Is that you? Do you believe me?"

Stace lowers her face to his and kisses his cheek. "It's Ruthie," she says. "I'm right here. I love you too."

Seb smiles. He doesn't draw another breath. Neither of us moves for a moment.

"Stace, you need to let the others in," I say finally, reaching for her hand as she rises to her feet. I pull her into a tight hug and then I'm running towards the green door.

29

He killed so many on the night he escaped. He wouldn't have been able to withstand the effects of such a rage; he hadn't properly come into his power, you see? He probably crawled away to die himself.

SAIGE, THE CITY

I enter a dark and narrow tunnel. My blood is pounding in time with my footsteps.

"Ruthie, wait." Dad is on my heels; he catches my arm. "Let me go first."

"She doesn't have a gun and she's alone," I say.

"We have no idea what she has, or who else might be waiting for her at the end of this tunnel," he insists.

"Fine. Give me the gun, then."

But he shakes his head. Dev appears behind Dad, fresh wounds on his face from his fight with the Giant.

"Let's go," he says, impatiently.

The tunnel is barely wide enough for two bodies, but Dad won't leave my side. We bump along, arm to arm.

Behind us we hear the heavy wooden door crash to the ground. Voices shout our names. Footsteps pound down the stone steps.

Zan and Noah appear in the gloom of the tunnel. They look bruised and torn. And victorious.

Noah is laughing. "It's over, Ruthie!" he shouts.

I catch Zan's eye as she steps forward, and I nod.

"She's down here, she escaped into this tunnel," I say.

And we're off again, more of us, moving faster now over the packed earth floor. The jagged rock walls feel like they're closing in. As we follow the curve of the tunnel, a bright light spills from a glass doorway in the distance. Something scuttles over my boot.

A voice, low and desperate, leaks into the tunnel. I freeze. Saige's voice.

"Is that *her*?" Noah whispers.

"Shhh," I say.

"I'm so sorry, Lily. So sorry," she's saying.

She sounds nothing like an ogre now.

"Forgive me. Forgive me."

I edge forward, but Dad takes my arm.

"Wait," he says. "Will you listen to me?"

I stand aside and he moves past me towards the dim shape moving around behind frosted glass, his weapon held high. There is another number panel set into the stone, but the door is slightly ajar. Dad slides his fingers around the frame, and pulls open the door.

It is almost impossible to make sense of what lies

beyond. Dev and Zan and Noah crowd in behind me and Dad. Their breaths come hot and fast, like mine.

Saige barely looks up when we enter the room. The light is dizzying, just like the Giften cells, but there are no cells—just a white room with panels of tiny green lights set into one wall. They flash on and off. Huge steel cabinets with glass doors line another wall. Bottles of clear liquid fill the shelves. The floor is white marble, covered with muddy, dusty footprints. There is another door at the back of the room; the exit and entrance to her lab.

What words would the Recorder have used to describe what is happening in the centre of this space? Suspended from four copper pipes fixed into the thick wooden ceiling beams is a glass tank of water, as long and as wide as a coffin. A naked girl floats fully immersed in glowing blue water. There are pads and tubes fixed to points on her shaved head and lean body. She looks only a little older than me.

Saige Corentin paces around the tank, her hands pressed to the glass. She is weeping, repeating the words we had heard earlier, *I'm sorry* and *Forgive me*.

Dad raises his gun and Zan her bow.

"Wait!" I shout and Saige snaps out of her trance. Seeing their weapons, her head dips to her chest. She holds up her hands, palms out. The smell of lavender wafts around the room.

"Do it," she whispers. "I'm ready."

"Wait!" I repeat as Zan draws back her arrow. "Don't you want to know what's going on here?" I point at the girl floating in the tank. "Who that is?"

Zan just shrugs. Her eyes narrow. "Whatever it is, whatever she's done to that poor girl, all her *shit*," she lifts her chin at Saige, "it's over, Ruthie." But her hands are trembling; she doesn't release the arrow, and I nudge the bow aside.

"*I* need to know what's going on, Zan," I say. "And so do you."

Saige is staring at me, her chest heaving, face red. Her yellow hair has come loose and hangs in damp ribbons across her shoulders. Her white clothes are smeared with dirt and someone's blood, the shiny boots are scuffed. She could be one of us now.

"This is Lily, my daughter." Her voice is thick with tears. She looks tiny, vulnerable, sad. The opposite of a monster. "We're waiting."

"Waiting for what?" I ask.

Saige presses her hands to the glass tank and stares at the girl within. "For Joshua," she says, her face crumbling.

I'm no hero from the old stories. I'm not going to kill the ogre or bring back our dead.

Logan isn't here, so I will do the work.

I turn to Zan. "I need to take Saige's record," I say.

*   *   *

Afternoon sunlight bathes our victory, the air is alive with birdsong, the wilderness smells sweet after the cells, after the lavender. But the survivors move slowly, pulling their loved ones away from their MAG killers, or collecting weapons, shoving them into canvas bags. They stop their work now and then to embrace, whispering words of support through watery smiles. At the edge of the wilderness, Stace has found Filip, her dad. They cry in each other's arms. And then a familiar voice tugs at my heart.

"Ruthie, well, well."

I bury my head into Old Pete's chest and weep.

"It's OK, it's OK," he says softly, stroking my hair. "You can go home now." He tips up my chin to meet his weary eyes and points to the line of MAGs bound and gagged along one wall of the house. "There are lessons on this battlefield, Ruthie," he says. "Victory alone is not enough. To really survive we must learn to live together." He takes in the courtyard, the house and the wilderness beyond with a wave of his hand. "There will always be people like them, but they are still part of this land."

I don't want to hear this right now. Maybe Old Pete is right, but all I see around me are the bodies of people who fought those who would snuff out our lives because of an impossible dream.

There is a different future ahead of us now, I think. Because now the whole of the North stands together. Ready for Southern strangers who might believe there's nothing here but defenceless farmers.

From across the courtyard the old man who helped us bury the bodies of our mutual enemies smiles and waves.

*   *   *

Saige is still alive, for now. I left her locked up in Dad's cell, sitting in the dirt, weeping for her dead daughter. I took the copper brooch from her shirt before I shoved her inside. This symbol of Giften power doesn't belong in her hands.

"Where's Joshie?" I asked her.

Very slowly she raised her head. "He escaped," she whispered.

"Then why didn't he come back to the Field?"

"I don't know," she said. "His power... it was too strong, and maybe miracles aren't ours to command after all."

Epilogue

I found my courage in the stories of others. In their words I heard my own voice; the relief of an abundant harvest before a cruel winter, the grief of bereavement, and the joy of new birth; all their sorrows and celebrations. And to these I will add new stories from our recent past; long narratives of fear and revenge, of despair and victory.

RUTHIE, THE FIELD

t's going to be a brutal winter. This thought and others, such as, *Nothing's changed* and *Everything's changed* fill my head as I bump the solar down the track through the Woods. In the three months I've been away, the forest floor has become a carpet of skeletal autumn leaves; the trees are naked. I smell the woodsmoke even before I see the chimneys pouring their yellow clouds.

My land has grown barren during our absence, as winter pressed her icy fingers to the ground. The veg has been pulled and the earth turned, ready for a new season of cropping. A shimmer of morning frost still rings the land.

The sky is uniform grey, blanketing my home in shadow, but behind the clouds I sense the sun.

I have missed the Field, and the missing is a pain I didn't know I was feeling until I returned and it vanished.

Cabin doors fling open as our convoy of two solars trundles towards the Shed.

"Give me a minute with Gemma? OK?" Dad asks. He's staring into the distance where Mum is leading Ant down the porch steps. He takes a deep breath and in seconds, he is sprinting across the Field.

*   *   *

He's coming home for the second time. In the months we've been away he's hardly talked about Mum, or about what happened in the cells. And he didn't seem in any hurry to leave the City.

We took a trip, just the two of us, further south to the coast. It was in the last days of autumn, just warm enough to still camp out. He taught me to swim in icy cold waters and how to throw a line into the sea and pull out supper. From the top of vast boulders we drew fat mackerel from the sea and roasted them over an open fire. I found my dad again; not the warrior who inspired an army, but the man who called me *chicken*, and messed up my hair. He was playful, funny, until Mum's name came up. Or Ant's. Then he would sigh and look away, slowly shaking his head.

"You regret it, don't you?" I asked him on the morning I drove us back to the City and the Base. "In the cells, killing Owen. Is that why you won't talk about it?"

"Do we have to do this?" he asked in a small voice, staring at his hands in his lap.

I wanted to scream at him then. *Yes, we have to.*

"Please, Dad," is what I said instead. "If you let it out, then it's not this big thing in your head. Like being Giften. I couldn't talk about it for a whole year and it was this awful secret, and now... now I can." I reach for his hand. "It's like I can breathe again."

"When did you get to be so wise, chicken?" He laughed, the skin crinkling at the corners of his eyes, around his mouth. He was getting older too and my heart gave a sudden pang for the man who had hoisted me on to his shoulders so I could pick my choice of late summer apples.

"Wise?" I laughed too, then grew serious. "When I had to leave the Field, I guess," I said. "But now it's time to go back. You will come back, won't you?"

He met my eyes, and nodded. "Of course I will."

*   *   *

In the middle of the Field, beside the Well, Mum and Dad hug; his shoulders heave in her arms, and she holds him. Ant tugs on his jacket. Dad wipes his eyes with his sleeve and bends over to pick up my brother and settle him on his shoulders. The sun emerges, for just a moment, lighting them up.

Stace, Dev and I sit silently in the solar, watching this scene unfold. I hear Stace sniff away her tears. Scottie reaches between the seats and coils a hand into my curls.

"Who's that with Dan?" he asks. The little boy likes to wind my perfect spirals around his small fingers, and then let them spring loose.

I turn towards him, take his face in my hands. "My mum. You're going to love her. And my baby brother," I tell him.

"What if they don't love me?" he asks.

"How could they not?" Stace says. "When you have such round, delicious cheeks?" She pulls him onto her lap and covers his face with kisses and salty tears.

Scottie giggles. Dev ruffles his hair.

"We have a gong too," he says, pointing to the steel sphere hanging above the Well. It catches the sun and glows.

*   *   *

Not all of us stayed in the City after the MAGs went down. Old Pete and Filip came back first, to spread the news of our victory and to reassure Mum and Jacintha and Mary that we were still alive. In truth, Dad wasn't the only one who wanted to delay his return. The Base was a wreck, a broken symbol of pain and power; I needed to turn it into something better.

As autumn turned the wild land red and then gold, I helped to clear the wilderness around the MAG headquarters. Sanctuary, Circle and the City dwellers worked side by side to turn it into hope, into cropland, to be nourished by the putrefying remains of the Offerings. It was hard, dirty work, but the hours and days sped by; my hands deep in the soil, encouraging new growth. My gift was stronger than ever. Under the fingers of the Giften, the winter meant nothing. We planted trees and potatoes, wildflowers and marrow. And it thrived.

When the wilderness had been cleared, we started on the Base; the glass doors replaced with wood, the Giften cells now a larder for the new food and the dungeons beneath the house a prison for unrepentant MAGs.

*   *   *

When I see Old Pete crossing the Field, the community following behind, I fling open the car door; the icy air hits me like a fist. I'm embraced again and again, wept over, welcomed. Over the shoulders of my friends, I watch Mum and Dad. Mum takes his arm and they turn around, find me in the crowd, and wave.

I leave behind talk of the battle, of Owen's death and Seb's betrayal, and I run towards my parents. Mum is crying again, holding me tight, trying to speak, but she can't.

"It's OK, Mum," I hiccup into her ear. "It's OK. We're all fine. I'm home." I reach for Dad's hand. "We're *all* home."

Ant is wailing. The sight of Mum's tears is too much for my baby brother. Dad lifts him off his shoulders and I sit him onto my hip.

"Oofie," he says, plunging sticky fingers into my hair.

There is a little boy, standing at the edge of the crowd, watching this tearful reunion. I beckon him over.

"Coming?" I yell.

Scottie is hoisted aloft by Noah who starts to run.

*   *   *

It only took a few days to get back into the rhythm of life in the Field, back to my chores. It will take longer to make this place a home for Scottie, but the signs are good. This evening, flushed pink and exhausted after a day of playing with the other smallies, he fell asleep on a mattress beside my bed, straight after supper.

Tonight, Dad and Noah and Dev are night-walking in the Woods, checking the traps. The cabin is warm, the stove a furnace of orange. I stare at Mum, tracing the faded engravings of our names on the table.

"Is Dad your One again?" I ask her.

Dad is in Seb's bed, but once or twice I have heard him cross the cold boards to her room, late at night.

"It's not that simple," she says, taking a deep breath.

"I need some time to work out what happened. What it was about Owen that…" She drifts off and her sentence hangs in the air, but Owen bewitched everyone, not just her.

Ant, still wide awake, is levering himself round the room, chair to table to chair to me, on the lumpy sofa. Mum looks out of the window, at the full moon hovering over the Field. She doesn't need to say any more. My baby brother climbs onto my lap and, with some help, jumps off. He does it again and again.

*   *   *

I don't share the Blazes with Noah, not yet. Instead, over the coming months we work our land in the Field to harvest winter vegetables and summer beans. We crack the ice on the woodland stream to quench our thirst. We coax tomatoes to life in the Shed. This *soldier* is becoming a friend. I'm aware I'm holding back; and he may be gone before I'm ready for more.

*   *   *

I buried Seb in the City dwellers' graveyard the day after the battle. Something tore in my heart as I recalled the tall, white-haired boy, blowing his fringe from his eyes. Field-raised, part of the same family, the same land under our fingernails and in our blood.

I found his knife in the pocket of an old jacket, with a whittled block of wood. It's a girl with wild curly hair, but her face is blank, a smooth veneer yet to be carved.

I came home without the boy who loved me, the boy who saved my life.

I slipped the wooden carving into the drawers of my nightstand. This is the Seb I want to remember, the boy whittling arrowheads by the Well on a hot summer day, his hair in his eyes.

Now he lies beside Lily Corentin and the dead Giften girl from cell six.

He wasn't the only one of us who died that day; Old Pete and Filip brought Logan's body back to the Field and now the Recorder is buried beneath the Giant Oak. Logan's work and my dreams are all I have left of my friend. It's always the same dream. Logan sits in the shade of the Giant Oak, beneath the wide canopy of branches on a spring day. The Recorder picks up a sheath of papers, licks the tip of a pencil and begins to write.

*   *   *

It is a bitter February morning, but the sun sits in a sky of pure, unblemished blue. From the window of the cabin, the Field is already at work. Old Pete emerges from the smokehouse, his arms full of brown paper parcels of meat. Dad and Filip drag a felled yew tree into the Shed, just as Lucia exits, her hands and clothes coated with flour. Smallies, bundled in warm clothing, gather kindling at the edge of the Woods. Scottie is amongst them, carefully laying dry twigs into a canvas bag.

I want to believe the worst is over. But I know there are others like Saige, who might decide, like her, that the North is just a Supply Run for Giften.

In the cells, she had asked me what was so special about the Field that it delivered such *prizes.*

It's something I have pondered on ever since she spoke those words.

Just two mornings ago, I was alone in the Blazes, pulling up parsnips. While my fingers ploughed the earth I thought about Joshie. He should have been working alongside me, pushing his hands deep into the soil to feel the itchy pinch of growth against his palms. I felt the prickle of new shoots deep in the earth, small miracles, tiny magics. Moments like these are our prizes.

And my heart swells when I sense them.

Small things, but they're enough to break your heart with their pure simplicity.

*   *   *

As winter beckons spring, I spend my evenings reading over the oral histories I recorded after the battle. The stories of the City dwellers, the Giften, and Circle. There is one I linger over night after night.

When the battle was over, Zan retreated into the arms of the Sanctuary, and cried with her people *for* her people. The Circle had rounded up the last of the MAGs and the worst seemed to be behind us. The bodies were being cleared and the communities had already started to dig their graves in the land beyond the wilderness. Dad and Filip and Old Pete were sharing a flask of liquor with Stace and Dev. Everyone was busy. It was time.

I went to her cell with paper and pencil.

In a voice which at first was hoarse and croaky, but became stronger and more arrogant as she recounted her story, Saige Corentin began to talk and I began to write.

I first came to the North many years ago...

TEEN AND YA FICTION

*Available and coming soon
from Pushkin Press*

HOTEL MAGNIFIQUE
Emily J. Taylor

BLADE OF SECRETS
MASTER OF IRON
DAUGHTER OF THE PIRATE KING
DAUGHTER OF THE SIREN QUEEN
THE SHADOWS BETWEEN US
WARRIOR OF THE WILD
Tricia Levenseller

BEARMOUTH
Liz Hyder

ECHO NORTH
Joanna Ruth Meyer

THE BEAST PLAYER
THE BEAST WARRIOR
Nahoko Uehashi

GLASS TOWN WARS
Celia Rees

THE DISAPPEARANCES
SPLINTERS OF SCARLET
Emily Bain Murphy

THE MURDERER'S APE
SALLY JONES AND THE FALSE ROSE
Jakob Wegelius

THE BEGINNING WOODS
Malcolm McNeill

THE WILDINGS
THE HUNDRED NAMES OF DARKNESS
Nilanjana Roy

THE RECKLESS SERIES

THE PETRIFIED FLESH · LIVING SHADOWS
THE GOLDEN YARN · THE SILVER TRACKS
Cornelia Funke

THE RED ABBEY CHRONICLES

MARESI · NAONDEL · MARESI RED MANTLE
Maria Turtschaninoff

THE SHAMER CHRONICLES

THE SHAMER'S DAUGHTER · THE SHAMER'S SIGNET
THE SERPENT GIFT · THE SHAMER'S WAR
Lene Kaaberbøl